TITLES BY NADIA LEE

AN IMPROPER DEAL
A HOLLYWOOD BRIDE
A HOLLYWOOD DEAL
THE BILLIONAIRE'S FORBIDDEN DESIRE
THE BILLIONAIRE'S FORGOTTEN FIANCÉE
THE BILLIONAIRE'S SECRET WIFE
THE BILLIONAIRE'S INCONVENIENT OBSESSION
THE BILLIONAIRE'S COUNTERFEIT GIRLFRIEND
LOVING HER BEST FRIEND'S BILLIONAIRE BROTHER
SEDUCED BY HER SCANDALOUS BILLIONAIRE
ROMANCED BY HER ILLICIT MILLIONAIRE CRUSH
PREGNANT WITH HER BILLIONAIRE EX'S BABY
PURSUED BY HER BILLIONAIRE HOOK-UP
TAKEN BY HER UNFORGIVING BILLIONAIRE BOSS

A HOLLYWOOD BRIDE

BILLIONAIRES' BRIDES OF CONVENIENCE

BOOK TWO

NADIA LEE

A Hollywood Bride
Copyright © 2016 by Hyun J. Kyung

This book is a work of fiction. The names, characters, places, and incidents are products of the writer's imagination or have been used fictitiously and are not to be construed as real. Any resemblance to persons, living or dead, actual events, locales or organizations is entirely coincidental.

All rights reserved. No part of this book may be reproduced, scanned, or distributed in any manner whatsoever without the prior written permission from the author except in the case of brief quotation embodied in critical articles and reviews.

To my readers.

ONE

Ryder

PAIGE REFUSES TO HAVE ME IN THE ROOM WITH her, insisting I stay outside. Does she blame me for what happened? I'm sure her fall had something to do with the bleeding. I can't think of any other reason she'd have issues, because up to that point she'd been thriving as a pregnant woman, glowing and happy. Not even any morning sickness.

If I hadn't rushed in at the club, Anthony wouldn't have pushed her. And so she wouldn't have fallen... I rub my face, then find a waiting room. A worn poster on the wall cites the dangers of cell phone use inside the hospital, something about how mobile devices interfere with medical equipment. I turn mine off. I don't want anything to mess with the care Paige is getting, but not having something to distract myself with is painful. There are so many ugly thoughts and possibilities going through my mind…and the atmosphere here doesn't help.

There's a difference between movie hospitals and real hospitals. Movie hospital sets smell normal. They don't give you that reflexive recoil in the deepest part of your heart. Real hospitals are the opposite. Decades of accumulated anxiety, misery, illness, and despair have settled in thick layers that no amount of chlorine can erase.

I park my butt in a molded plastic chair designed to be both uncomfortable and ugly and pull my baseball cap down. A large pair of dark sunglasses covers most of my face, but it's my busted lip that seems to be making people hesitant to assume I am who I am—Ryder Reed, one of the hottest movie stars in Hollywood. I've done some action flicks, but I've never gotten into a public fistfight.

Still, curious gazes slide over me. I ignore them. I like to engage with the public and my fans—actors are mostly extroverts—but only on my own terms, and certainly not in some dingy ER waiting room.

The clock on the wall ticks interminably, and my eyes gradually become gritty and unfocused. And my ass is getting numb. Damn it, how long does it take to see if Paige's all right? I guess the doctors want to be thorough and run all the appropriate tests.

Unless… Nausea roils in my belly. Unless the unthinkable has happened.

"Hey, are you that movie star?"

The boyish voice startles me out of my reverie. A child who looks like an animated marshmallow stands in front of me. A dingy white t-shirt and faded jeans don't improve his appearance. He's short enough that even seated my upper stomach is at his eye level. He's five…maybe six.

"My brother said you are," the boy adds, when I don't respond.

Another boy joins him. He looks like the first, except slightly bigger and rounder and whiter. He's so pale he practically glows under the neon lighting.

He pokes the smaller boy. "Told ya, dumbass. That's Ryder Reed."

"Did you get into a fight?" the younger boy asks, widening his eyes.

The older boy is entirely too gleeful. "Of course, he did. Look at his mouth. Bam!" he shouts as he makes a punching motion.

He's drawing attention to me, and I grimace. Where the hell is his mother?

The bigger one points at my mouth. "He's here to get treated for that lip."

"Who did you fight?" the younger boy asks.

The older boy says, "It's gotta be that girl."

"What girl?"

"The fat one. She came in all bloody."

As ridiculous as their conversation is, the muscles in my face start to tighten. This is how rumors start, and I need to put an end to the bullshit right now. "It wasn't the girl. I do not hit women."

"That's not true." The older boy sniffs disdainfully, his mouth set in a knowing sneer that seems wrong on such a young face. "I watched *Lethal Connection*. You fought that chick, then punched her and stuff. Man, that was so awesome! The bitch went down!"

"Yeah!" The younger kid pumps a fist above his head. "Bitches need to go down!"

I stare at the children, horrified at their language and stunned that they've seen that movie. It was rated R for…well, pretty much everything. Violence, excessive nudity, profanity. You name it.

I lean forward. "Okay, c'mere." They come in closer. "First, you shouldn't say the b-word. It's not nice. Second, she wasn't a normal person, but a genetically enhanced humanoid cyborg."

The younger kid lowers his voice to a stage whisper. "Then why was the girl who came with you bleeding? If you didn't knock her out?"

His brother is still going off. "I bet she was being all *bitchy* and had to be put in her place."

I feel like there's a ticking bomb in my head. Kids this young pick up stuff from their parents. If this is their attitude, maybe it explains why their mother is nowhere to be seen. Or maybe they picked it up from R-rated movies they should never have been allowed to watch in the first place.

I make a *time out* gesture with my hands. "Listen, both of you. You can't talk about women like that."

The squishy nostrils flare on the older kid's flushed face. "Why not?"

I grind my teeth. If this bratty kid were mine…

When I don't bother to answer, he gets in my face. "*Why the hell not?*"

"I told you: because it's not nice. Now, go find your mother and leave me alone, or I'm going to call the cops," I say, giving them Serious Look Number Two. I'm not going to do that, of course. But I figure it should scare them.

It doesn't.

Both boys start screaming and yelling. My head hurts even more, and I'm ready to call somebody—anybody—to come take these mini-psychos away from me.

A woman hustles toward me. She is obviously the prototype for the two marshmallow children, except larger and female. "Hey, what did you do to my kids?"

What the hell? "Nothing. They came over to talk to me. Which you would've noticed if you'd been watching them."

She puts her hands on her hips. "What are you implying? I'm a good mother!" She raises her voice. "I take care of my kids, I watch 'em, and I teach 'em right!"

"You mean like letting them see movies like *Lethal Connection*?"

"This is America. Freest country in the world, and I'm entitled to let my kids watch whatever they want. I'm not some brainwashed statist!"

Clearly, I need to exit this conversation. At the same time, I'm stressed and about to erupt because her annoying kids think it's okay to bother me when I'm doing my best not to talk to anybody. My fame does not give them the right to intrude into my private life. "Just take your kids and go away. Please."

But Mrs. Marshmallow isn't going to leave it alone. She starts to get in my face and scream hysterically about what a fit mother she is. She even demands that I apologize. *For what?* I haven't said a single thing that isn't true, and it's not my fault she lets her kids watch R-rated movies and use foul language. The volume of her voice cannot make up for her lack of manners and common sense.

Unfortunately, her hysterics are drawing attention. I grit my teeth. Add this to the list of reasons I hate hospitals.

A young nurse comes over. She's a tall, attractive blonde with light brown eyes and full lips that are currently turned down in disapproval. Still, she maintains her composure. Her ponytail swings as she turns to the loud woman first. "Ma'am, you need to be quiet. Or I'll have to have security escort you out of the building until you calm down."

The nurse might as well have tossed a bucket of gasoline over fire. The woman goes absolutely crazy. Spittle flies from her mouth, and her thick neck and cheeks go a deep shade of red even as the rest of her stays fish-belly white.

Another nurse comes up, fifty-something, and lays a gentle hand on my shoulder. "I'm very sorry, sir. I know you've been waiting a long time. Can you come with me for a moment?"

My gut tightens. I can't read her expression, but it's got to be bad.

I follow her down a long hallway. My feet feel like lead. I think of all the comforting words I need to say to Paige. "I'm so sorry" seems pathetically inadequate.

We come to the end of the hall and the nurse opens the door. I walk in, ready for some serious consolation action, then stop.

The room is empty. There are two cheap plastic chairs and a rectangular Formica table. No windows. As I make a slow circle in the center, my brows crease together. The place looks like something out of a spy flick—a torture room where the villain attempts to beat the truth out of the hero. All it needs is a lamp swinging over one of the chairs, casting dramatic shadows.

"It might be better if you wait here. More privacy. I'm sorry we don't have someplace nicer, but we're overflowing and understaffed right now."

"Where's Paige?"

"Paige?"

"My fiancée. Where is she?"

"I don't know, but I'll check."

She turns, about to leave, then pauses. "Would you like some ice?" She indicates her lip with a sympathetic look.

"If you don't mind. Sure."

It doesn't take long before she returns with the ice and cleans the crust of blood and other gunk off my lip. Her touch is professional, which I appreciate. I don't have the energy or patience to deal with stalkerish behavior. And fan-stalkers are everywhere.

She gives me the bag of ice. "Just hold it on there. Should make you feel better."

"Thanks. And can you let me know as soon as you get an update on Paige?"

"Of course."

When the door closes behind her, I numb my lip with the ice and will Paige and the baby to be all right.

Paige

RYDER'S HERE. IN THE BUILDING.

One part of me wants him by my side, but another doesn't. We haven't talked about—much less resolved—anything. This isn't even his baby, but he held my hand in the ambulance and whispered soothing words I couldn't comprehend over the roaring in my head. I'd rather not put him in a position where he feels forced into providing me with empty words of comfort and meaningless pats on my shoulder…but I still want him here.

The clock on the wall says it's only been hours, but everything seems to have happened over years. I hate being alone with nothing but my fears, anxiety stretching every second into something interminable.

I tense as a doctor finally walks in with a thick folder and chart.

He's surprisingly young, with gel-spiked black hair and dark eyes. A hoop hooks around the highest point of his left eyebrow. Sniffing, he runs a finger under his nose and flips through the papers.

Except for the lab coat, he looks nothing like a doctor should. Sweat slickens my palms. "Is everything all right?" I ask, unable to wait a second longer for information on my baby.

His head snaps up. "What? Yes. Yes, your baby is fine."

Sagging with relief, I lay my hands over my belly. *Thank god.*

"By the way, I'm Dr. Min. I don't recall if I introduced myself."

I give him a neutral smile. Even if he did, I probably wouldn't remember. Everything since I got out of Ryder's Ferrari with my bloody skirt is sketchy, like I experienced it through a dense fog.

He continues, "But you should still be careful. Your blood pressure is a little high for my liking. That and this incident—plus your weight—make this a high-risk pregnancy."

High risk. The words echo in my ears as I stare at the doctor. He's not the first medical professional to tell me to watch my weight, but it's the first time I've had somebody tell me it might harm the baby. I try to speak, but my mouth is so dry I can barely vocalize. I clear my throat and try again. "Are you telling me I should diet?"

He gives me a look. "I know how futile it is to tell a pregnant woman she needs to diet. Hard enough normally, and a lot worse when you have cravings. But next time, you should consider losing some weight before getting pregnant."

I cringe inwardly at the matter-of-fact way he speaks. I know it's nothing personal, but somehow I feel like I've failed my baby. I stroke my stomach guiltily.

"Take it easy, and make an appointment to see your regular doctor as soon as possible. Dr. Silverman, right?"

I nod.

"She's good." He grins unexpectedly, and suddenly looks like a teenage boy. "Any questions?"

I look down, then raise my eyes to meet the doctor's. "Did you…see my fiancé outside?"

"No. But I'll ask a nurse. Anything else?"

I shake my head.

He leaves, his step brisk. I'm sure he has hundreds of other patients.

I pull up my phone and text Ryder.

Sorry it was such a long wait. I'm done. Ready to go?

I wait a while, but no response. I text him again just in case.

More time, and still nothing. I know he has his phone; he used it to call nine-one-one earlier.

A hole grows in my chest. Did he just…go home? I asked him to wait outside even though I knew he wanted to come in with me. To be honest, I would've preferred that he be there for the consultation. But there's this small part of me that doesn't want to be dependent on him. He's only marrying me so he can get his grandfather's painting.

And it's only going to be for a year.

I could contact my stepsister, but that would create problems. I still don't know what to tell her about my scandalous situation with the sex tape. And I haven't told her about my pregnancy. I don't want to say a word about it, not even to her, since Ryder and I are planning to make an announcement after the wedding.

There's a quick knock, and a uniformed chauffeur I've never seen before walks into the room. He's in a black suit with a heavily starched white shirt and a pair of white gloves. Silver roots show at the temples, and the left side of his face is slightly darker than the right. "Ms. Johnson," he begins, his voice courteous. "My name is Perry Finds. Mr. Reed sent me to pick you up."

"Oh." I guess Ryder sent him for me. "You didn't happen to bring me a change of clothes, did you?"

He pauses. "I'm afraid not, miss."

"I…um…soiled my skirt." I clear my throat.

"Of course," he says, as though bleeding all over one's skirt is an everyday occurrence. He shrugs out of his jacket and hands it to me. "Will this be acceptable to cover it up?"

Startled, I look at the proffered garment and him. He doesn't look any less formal without his jacket, and I feel awkward, but beggars can't be choosers. "Thank you." I take his jacket. The fabric isn't rich, but it's not cheap either.

"I'll wait for you in the hall. Please take your time."

He walks out, and I quickly change into my outfit and wrap the jacket around my waist to cover the bloodstains. They'll probably never come out, and I'm going to have to throw the skirt away. But I'm too grateful to care. My child is going to be okay. That's all that matters.

I take my purse and step out. The chauffeur is waiting, standing with hands clasped and feet spread.

"I need to fill out some paperwork for the discharge and instruct the hospital where to send the bills."

"No need to worry about that. Everything's been taken care of."

Typical Ryder: take care of the hospital bills, but forget a fresh change of clothes for me. He isn't used to handling such details. That used to be my job, but he doesn't have me doing it anymore. I doubt his new assistant knows what's going on. It takes a while for people to earn his trust.

Perry puts a hand at my elbow and escorts me outside. On the curb is an idling black Bentley. It's so waxed and shiny I can use it as a mirror.

He opens the door for me, and I slide in. Then I stop short.

Julian Reed is in the car. He moves toward the window, giving me ample space on the luxurious leather bench—a subtle dig at my size? Although he's Ryder's father, they don't share many similarities. He is blond, while Ryder is dark-haired. He is of average height, while Ryder is tall. He is petty and snide, while Ryder is not.

"Mr. Reed."

"Hello, Paige." He smiles, but the expression isn't particularly welcoming. He tilts his head at the driver. "Perry, let's go."

The door shuts behind me with a solid *thunk*.

TWO

Ryder

THE CHAIRS IN THIS ROOM ARE JUST AS UNCOMfortable as the ones in the waiting room. The harsh fluorescent lighting doesn't help either.

It really does have an effect. I feel like some kind of criminal, waiting in an interrogation room for the cops to question me.

When I stand up, my bones creak like they belong to an eighty-year-old. I *feel* eighty after sitting in that horrible chair for hours. I should go check up on Paige. This is taking way too long, and I have to know she's going to be all right.

The door opens, and the nurse who told Mrs. Marshmallow to behave slips inside. Her golden hair is down, curling around her shoulders. She seems a bit taller, and I realize she's swapped out her shoes. A pair of heels encases her feet. She closes the door behind her and faces me.

The light shines directly on her features. Her powder is fresh, and a fresh coat of red lipstick glistens on her lips. In an apparent attempt to make her eyes look larger, she's put on layers of mascara until there's more makeup than eyelashes. A cheap perfume stings my nose, and all my internal alarm bells go off.

There's no way she's here to update me on Paige.

"Finally!" She takes the front of her blouse with both hands in a Superman gesture and pulls. The cheap fabric gives way, and I bite back a groan. *What the fuck?*

"You have no idea how serendipitous it was that you showed up right after I spent an hour shopping at Victoria's Secret." *Serendipitous. Do all nurses talk like that?*

She licks her lips. "It's as if the universe wants us to be together."

"No, it really doesn't." I try to walk around her. I have zero interest in hooking up with anybody. But the woman is not at all amenable to moving away. The ripped shirt reveals tits that don't even bounce when she steps closer to press them against me.

"You know you want this…" Her breathing grows louder as she cups her silicon boobs.

They're too large for her narrow body. "I've studied your type. You like them with big breasts. And blonde."

She is somewhat correct. I also like women with an ass, not something that looks like it's been run over by a steamroller a couple of times. "Lady, get the fuck away from me before I call the cops."

"Oh, you won't."

I give her my best level stare. "Try me."

"Is it because I'm not her?"

"What the hell are you talking about?"

"Is it because I'm not a fat cow like her?" Her voice is getting loud, and anger lends a razor glint to her eyes. *Oh boy*.

"Paige is not a cow. She's my fiancée."

"She's fucking fat! What the hell do you see in her? Why would you want her when you can have me? Haven't you read all the letters I sent?" She drops her skirt, revealing thigh-highs and a lacy garter belt.

I've always thought nice lingerie improved a woman. But she's an exception.

When I don't react in the way she obviously expected, she spreads and bends her knees. The lewd gesture shows her panties—apparently made crotchless with scissors before she came inside the room—and her private parts.

Jesus, my eyes. Maybe one of the doctors here can induce strategic amnesia.

Crimson mottles her face and neck. "Why don't you want this? Why don't you want me? Can't you see I'm all wet?"

Good fucking god. She's gotta be off her meds. What the fuck is wrong with the hospital that they hired unhinged people like her? I reach for my phone. "I'm calling the cops. I've had enough."

She lunges for me. "I am the Cinderella you need. I've waited so long for you!"

I sidestep her. High heels are not conducive for physical activity, and I've learned some moves from doing my own stunts in action flicks. She goes past and I open the door.

"I need security!" I yell into the hall. "Now!"

"No!" The psycho nurse comes after me, but she's still hampered by her footwear. The cheap shoes clack on the linoleum. She hasn't even bothered to put her clothes back on.

What a damn spectacle.

A nurse walking by gasps, her eyes wide.

"Get security," I tell her. "*Right now*. Unless you want to hear from my lawyer."

Near-Naked Nurse grabs my wrist. "Ryder! My prince!"

Yeesh. I yank my arm away. Her grip is stronger than expected, and it takes some effort to get free.

"Why are you doing this?" Tears gather in her eyes. "Do you have any idea how long I've waited for you to realize the truth about us?"

"The only truth is that you need some serious help." I stay in the hall, trying to ensure she stays here rather than wander off to other areas with young children. But she's seriously making my skin crawl.

Her mouth pinches until the lips form a tight, ugly line. "It's all that bitch's fault! I'm gonna get her, you know!"

"Listen to me carefully. There is nothing between us. *Nothing*. If we were stranded on Mars, I wouldn't want you. Understand?"

"You *asshole!* I sent you *gifts!*"

You and ninety-nine percent of my sociopath psycho fans.

She jumps suddenly and rams her face into my biceps. Her teeth cut into my skin, and I shove her away, palm to her forehead.

"What the hell?" I look down and see blood well in an arc.

A couple of men in dark blue uniforms show up. Thankfully they're young and seem to be in good shape. Now they can deal with this crazy woman.

At the sight of them, she tries to latch onto me. "No! Make them go away. They're here to take me away from you!"

She is crazy. Abso-fucking-lutely off her rocker. "Watch the teeth. This psycho bit me!" I tell the guards.

"Ryder! How can you betray me like this? It's all her fault. *That witch!*"

The guards close in, and she starts running. She doesn't get very far before they catch her.

The nurse I saw before comes over. "Are you all right?" she asks.

"Yeah." I've had worse. At least the crazy nurse didn't try to run me over with a Jeep. "Does she actually work here?"

The corners of her mouth droop. "Unfortunately, yes. I'm… I don't even know what to say. She's always been a big fan of yours, but none of us had any idea…" She shakes her head. "We should look at that bite."

"It's nothing."

"No, it's not. She broke the skin." The nurse frowns, looking more closely at my arm. "Human bites can be more dangerous than dog bites. All kinds of bacteria in the mouth. At least you're in the right place."

I sigh. She's right. The smart play is to get it looked at, just in case. Psycho-nurse could have rabies for all I know. "Is this going to take long? I really need to see my fiancée."

"Oh, I meant to tell you. She's been discharged."

"*What?*" I stare at the nurse. "She doesn't have a ride."

The nurse gives me a professionally sympathetic look. "Might have called a taxi. I don't really know. Why don't you call her and ask?"

"I don't get it. Is she safe? Shouldn't you keep her here overnight for, I don't know, observation or something? She almost lost her baby today."

"I'm sorry, but I don't have that information. I need to check the records."

How the fuck can she know that they let Paige go, but not know if my fiancée is okay or not? With an effort, I rein myself in. Yelling at this nurse won't solve anything. It probably wasn't even her who processed the paperwork for Paige.

I turn my phone on. The latest text is from my agent Mira. *Are you at a hospital? The story's trending on Twitter.*

God, I hate social media.

There are also several earlier texts, all of them from Paige. The last one is fifteen minutes old. I start typing.

※

Paige

THE CAR IS MOVING ALONG SLOWLY IN THE LA traffic. I look outside and notice that Julian's driver is taking a roundabout way to Ryder's mansion.

But I should've known that Julian didn't show up just to give me a ride.

"Here." Julian twists the cap off a mini bottle of water—the kind you'd normally find on an airplane—and hands it to me. "You should stay hydrated."

I take it and have a sip. Then I realize I'm thirsty. I haven't had anything to drink since I went to Anthony's club. "Thanks. But I'm sure you aren't giving me a ride just to make sure my fluid levels are okay."

"You've probably only heard negative things about me from my son, but I'm not the villain here, Paige."

Suuuuuure. "Then why are you having me followed?

"Having you followed?" He raises an eyebrow. The angle of his raised brow is exactly the same as Ryder's when he cocks his, and it disorients me for a moment. They look so different, I sometimes actually forget he's Ryder's father. "What do you mean?"

"How else did you know to find me at the hospital?"

My phone pings with a new text. I'm about to ignore it, but Julian says, "You should answer that. Might be important."

Well. If he insists...

It's from Ryder. *Where are you?*

On my way home.

Cab?

No. I start to type *I'm in a car with your father*, then hit delete. That won't go over well. My head hurts. I don't want to have any kind of serious conversation about his father or anything else via text right now. *I'll explain later.*

Okay.

I drop the phone back into my purse.

"Who was that?" Julian asks.

"Ryder."

"Hmm. Guess he wants to know who's giving you a ride home."

"Actually you can take me to my car. I left it at Z." I doubt Ryder remembered to fetch it. I want my Altima back.

Julian gives me a speculative look. "I can manage that." He hits the intercom button and instructs his driver to take us to the popular club. "As for your worry that I'm stalking you, I don't need to bother with such mundane things. There's this thing now called the Internet. Surely you've heard of it."

I don't buy that one bit. "I'm not famous enough to warrant an article."

"Social media is more or less instantaneous, and you are a person of great interest now, especially with that unfortunate tape of yours."

"It's not my tape," I mutter as my face heats.

Did Julian watch that too? My skin crawls at the idea.

He shrugs. "There were pictures of you and Ryder." He looks at my belly. "How's the baby? Still kicking?"

I tense. He's got to be fishing. I wish I could check my own social media to see what's being said, but doing that would give myself away. Assuming I could even find the tweets and mentions about my hospital visit, of course. There's probably more stuff about that damn sex tape. People love to say horrible things about women when things like this happen. So instead I play dumb. "What baby?"

"The Internet said you were bleeding. I'm pretty certain it isn't due to a feminine hygiene product malfunction."

You could fry a steak on my face now. I always knew how difficult it was to maintain privacy in Hollywood, but this is ridiculous. I'm nobody famous.

"Don't look at me like I eat babies for breakfast. I only do that with other people's babies, and this one's going to be my grandchild."

It's his version of a joke, but I shudder. If his actions as a father are anything to go by, he's going to make a horrible grandparent.

Julian taps his lower lip. "I wondered why you

agreed to marry my son. Ryder isn't the sort to be okay with commitment, and most likely he's going to cheat on you. No matter how desperate he is for the portrait, he is who he is…and you're not his type."

He isn't saying anything I don't know. When Ryder makes love to me, I can almost believe he really cares about me, but I'm also aware that all this is transient. Ryder's mansion isn't my home, even if I do live there at the moment. I'm just a temporary guest.

"I always had the impression you were too sensible to fall for my son. If you were so stupid as to love him, he would've fired you a long time ago." He regards me coolly. "Your wedding is in three weeks. I presume it's still on? Or have things changed because of the tape?"

His blunt questions stun me. I haven't given any thought to the wedding since the sex tape was released. My mind has been more obsessed with the fact that my parents saw me naked. That Ryder saw me having sex with my ex. And that millions of people out there are watching me on that horrible tape Shaun made without my consent. The enormity of the violation leaves me shaking all over again.

"Well, whatever the date, I want you to go ahead," he says. "Proceed as planned with the wedding. Then, on that day, you're to leave my son at the altar."

I gasp. "That will completely humiliate him!"

Julian looks at me like I'm a dim-witted child. "Well, of course."

"Why are you doing this? Why do you hate Ryder so much?"

"I don't hate him."

"Really? Is that why every time he releases a new movie you send a binder full of negative reviews? Of all the petty things to—"

"It's for his own good. He needs to learn respect and humility."

Is this guy serious? "You should be proud of him. He got to where he is without your help."

"Is that what he told you?" Julian's mouth twists. "Luck is nothing to be proud of. Nor is winning the genetic jackpot. Do you think it was through his own effort that he was born to me and his mother—to the best families in America? Or that it was through his own effort that he's as handsome as he is? Of course not. He got most of his looks from me and perhaps a bit from his mother."

I snort. If Julian really believes that, he's deranged.

He continues, "And it's not through his own effort that a bloodsucker like that agent of his discovered him and is using him to line her own pockets."

"You don't understand him at all. He's smart, and works incredibly hard."

Julian laughs until tears roll down his cheeks. Gasping for air, he wipes them away with an index finger. "That's one of the funniest things I've ever heard. Oh, how I wish Geraldine's mother were here. She always thought Ryder was slightly retarded."

My jaw slackens. "What?"

"You didn't know that? Shirley Pryce, the Matriarch," he says, making finger quotes in the air and raising his eyebrows in mock awe, "considered Ryder too stupid to be a Pryce. Except he was one, much to her displeasure, and he didn't even bother to go to college despite her insistence that he do so. I bet it killed that old bat she couldn't deny he was one of them." His mouth curls into a sneer. "He has the Pryce profile." He hands me another mini-bottle of water. When I don't take it, he shrugs and drinks it himself. "Now, let's get down to business. I can double whatever Ryder's promised you. And you won't have to tie yourself to a man who probably hates you right now for that sex tape. It's one thing to know your fiancée isn't a virgin. It's quite another to see her fucking another man."

I tighten my hands into fists and force myself to breathe calmly. It won't do me any good to get myself worked up over Julian's words. "I have no intention of betraying him. And I don't care how big the carrot you're dangling is. You think you're the first person to offer me money?"

"No. But I'm quite sure that I'm the first person to tell you that if sweetness doesn't work, I'm willing to be more drastic."

"Are you threatening me?"

"Oh, no. If I become drastic, my dear, everyone will get hurt, not just you."

The absolute conviction in his words shakes me. The man is enough of a megalomaniac to believe he's entitled to get what he wants, using whatever means necessary. And his threat to hurt the people around me is delivered in such a calm way that I start to wonder if he's sane.

"If you go after people I care about, I will fight back," I say.

"Then you are a fool," he purrs like an amused predator toying with its prey. "And have no sense of self-preservation."

I almost crush the water bottle in my hand. Julian may be right about my sense of self-preservation or lack thereof, but I won't just sit back and let him walk all over me.

Apparently having made his point, he doesn't bother to talk to me for the rest of the ride. I watch the scenery go by outside. The silence is better than his smugness and threats.

Finally we make it to Z. Fortunately, my car's still in the parking lot…and it's intact. You never know in L.A.

I get out before Julian's driver can open the door. The man still hustles over. I start to pull off his jacket, but he shakes his head, gesturing for me to keep it.

Julian says, "It was lovely talking with you, my dear. Take your time and think about what I said."

Over my dead body. The driver shuts the Bentley door and the car pulls away.

I unlock my Altima and sit in the driver's seat. I grip the steering wheel and immediately let go; it's hot enough to grill beef.

Okay. Roll down the windows, crank the A/C. In a few moments it's cool enough that I can sit and actually think about what Julian said. First decision: I'm not going to do what he asked. It's wrong, and Ryder doesn't deserve to be treated like that.

But Julian also made some good points. Based on what's happened since the sex tape was released, it's clear Ryder doesn't trust me. A trusting man wouldn't have lashed out at me the way he did. And I don't know if I can go ahead and marry him if he distrusts me, even if it's only for a year.

I sit for a while with the A/C blowing, mulling things over. But my phone finally beeps, pulling me out of my thoughts.

It's a text from Ryder.

Are you okay? Where are you?

Just getting my car. Are you home?

Yes. I freaked when you weren't here. You left before I did.

I'll be there soon. Will you be home when I get back?

Yes.

I toss the phone on the passenger seat and start the car. It's time Ryder and I have a talk.

THREE

Paige

When I arrive at the mansion, security opens the gate immediately. It's amazing how different the place feels now, even though it's been less than twenty-four hours since I was last here. The pool looks like polished onyx, cold and unfathomable. Even the flowers seem unfriendly.

By the time I park my car and get inside the house, I'm starving. The smell of food reminds me that I haven't eaten anything since breakfast. I really need to do better. Even if I'm stressed—or in a hospital—my baby still has needs.

His feet bare, Ryder walks over when he sees me. Security has notified him of my arrival; you can't see people coming in and out of the house from the kitchen or the living room. His dark hair is slightly damp, as though he's just gotten out of the shower. He's in a white T-shirt and dark denim shorts. Despite the ultra-casual look, he is stunning, his blue eyes focused and his mouth set in a small smile. If I didn't know him as well as I do, I might've thought he was happy to see me. But the curvature of his lips is too perfect, an exact replica of the expression I've seen on the big screen so many times.

He gives me a tight hug, burying his face in my hair. "Next time, page me. You had me worried when you disappeared."

I tighten my arms around him. When we're like this, I can almost believe everything's fine between us. "Okay."

A fresh bandage covers his left bicep. "What's that?" I don't remember Anthony *cutting* Ryder during their fight…

"Nothing." He clicks his teeth once and opens his mouth as though he wants to say something more. But then he shakes his head. "I had a chef make some salad and chicken Parmesan. Your mother told me it's your favorite."

He spoke with my mom. It had to have been after my hospital visit. "Did you tell her about…"

"No. But she'll hear about it soon enough." His eyes drop to the jacket wrapped around my waist. "What's that?"

"Just something I borrowed to cover the stains on my skirt. I'll get it dry cleaned and sent back."

"I'll have housekeeping handle it." He clears his throat. "Are you all right? Everything good with, you know. The baby?" Tension pinches his forehead and puts brackets around his mouth.

"We're both fine. Don't worry." Unable to help myself, I put a hand to his cheek. The lines between his eyebrows ease, and I wish I'd asked him to stay by my side at the hospital. He's a great actor, but I don't think he's faking it.

Looking into his eyes, the weight of Julian's proposition bears down on me. I should tell Ryder about it, but not right now. It will only enrage him, and right at the moment I want some peace and quiet. The day's been exhausting, with too many ups and downs. "I need to change."

I start up the stairs. My pelvis throbs, making me wince. The pain is probably going to get worse before it gets better. If I remember correctly, it always hurts more the next day. But I'm not going to take any medication. Chemicals, even if they're medicinal, probably aren't good for a developing fetus.

"Paige, wait." He makes his way toward me. He puts a hand on my pelvis and feels around, like he wants to make sure nothing's broken. "Did they check this out?"

"Yes. It's fine." I grip his hand, stopping the tactile inquisition. "If you really want to help, escort me up the stairs."

And he does. Once we reach the end of the hall where our side-by-side suites are located, we stop. "You need any help changing?" he asks.

"No. I'll be fine. Thanks."

I walk into my suite and close the door, grateful for the privacy. After kicking off my sandals and dumping my clothes—including Julian's driver's jacket—in a hamper, I change into loose gray cotton pants and an off-white tank top with pink smiley faces. I need a bit of happy in my life, and the tank top's never failed to cheer me up…until now.

In the mirror, a haggard blonde with dark circles and brackets around her mouth stares back.

"Come on, Paige. You have on your happy tank. Smile."

I slap my cheeks lightly to put some color into them and pull my lips back. Now I look like a zombie that just heard a really good joke.

So far Ryder's been solicitous. It's like the medical emergency totally changed his attitude. Until I started bleeding, he was upset about the sex tape and my seeing Anthony.

But I'm also painfully aware that it's all just temporary. That tape isn't going away. It's going to be in our faces until the wedding three weeks from now. Actually probably longer, unless somebody else does something crazy to get the media's attention.

Putting on a neutral expression, I bunch my limp hair into a simple ponytail, then go out into the hall. Ryder straightens away from the wall at the sight of me.

"Dinner's being served in my suite," he says.

It is? "The dining room's okay."

"Yeah, but it's just the two of us. And I thought it might be easier if you didn't have to go up and down the stairs." His gaze drops to my pelvis for a moment. "You take anything for that?"

I shake my head. "I'm fine."

We go into his room. It's larger and more opulent than any hotel suite, with a bedroom and a separate seating area, plus a walk-in closet that's bigger than most studio apartments. I see a table and chairs that weren't there before; housekeeping must've set them up.

Ryder pulls out a chair for me and I sit, murmuring my thanks. Our dinner is a simple affair with tossed garden salad, freshly baked rolls and my favorite chicken Parmesan. Taking a deep breath, I pick up my fork and brace myself for the next few hours.

Ryder

I sit on Paige's right. We eat in silence. It's partly because I'm hungry, but also because I want to act like the issues between us—the ones that made us raise our voices at each other—don't exist. Easy to do if I keep my focus on how close she came to losing her baby. I don't think I'll ever forget the sight of that blood on her skirt.

The food is fantastic, as usual. My chef spares no expense getting the best ingredients, and today's no exception. I try to pretend that this is like any of the dinners Paige and I have had before. When we traveled for work, we generally ate together. I hate eating alone, and she kept me company.

A pang pierces me. The good old times are never coming back. Things are too different now.

"Is there anything we need to do to make sure…you know." I gesture at her belly.

"No. I just need to take it easy. And make an appointment to see Dr. Silverman as soon as possible."

The definitive tone of her voice says the topic's over, even though the soft frown on her face says there is more to it than what she's sharing. If she's trying to make clear how much she wants to keep me out, she's doing a damn good job.

The next few minutes pass in a silence that feels like a boulder pressing down on me. Paige's shoulders are sloped down, her spine half-slumped into a C. She's feeling it as much as me.

I make small talk about some scripts I've been reviewing. She nods at the right times, but there's no spark in her eyes. After a while, I give up.

A small bit of annoyance knots inside my gut. We still haven't talked about what's important—the sex tape, her visit with Anthony, how we should handle everything. I don't want to talk about any of that anyway until she's feeling better. But it's hard when she's shutting me out, acting like she's some kind of martyr.

It's not my fault things are the way they are.

We finish our meals at the same time. She places her utensils back on the table precisely so, as if everything depends on their proper alignment.

"Thank you. It was very good," she says, then starts to stand. She doesn't even straighten to her full height before she cries out and almost crumples. I'm out of my seat and holding her in an instant. She's flushed, and the knuckles of her hand are white on the back of her chair.

"Are you okay?"

"Yes. It was nothing. Sorry." She exhales a long breath and doesn't quite meet my eyes.

Right. I pick her up. Even as her arms tighten around my neck, she says, "Put me down. You're going to hurt yourself."

I give her a look. "As if."

"But I'm…heavy." The last word is spoken so softly, I almost miss it.

I don't bother to answer. I'm not going to hurt myself carrying her to bed. Besides, it's nice to hold a woman who doesn't feel like she's going to break in half if I breathe wrong. Anger fills me as I remember how Anthony pushed her in the middle of the fight. Even though she acts like it was nothing, I know the fall hurt her. She's been walking like an old woman ever since.

Despite her asking me to stay away, I should've been with her. That way, she would've gotten the care that she needs for her injuries. She might be too focused on the baby to demand more for herself, but not me.

I place her gently in the middle of my bed. Biting her lower lip, she looks away as I peel her pants and underwear off. I don't care if she's uncomfortable, as long as she lets me check her out.

I suck in a breath. There's a dark reddish blossom on her left hip that looks like a lurid flower. It's the size of an ostrich egg and is going to deepen into black and purple tomorrow.

"Damn."

"It's really not that bad." Her voice is light, but shaky.

"You should've said something to the doctor. They would've given you something."

"Ryder, no. No painkillers. Nothing that's going to risk the baby."

I get that, I do. Still, I'll be lying if I said I'm okay with this.

"Don't move." I point a finger at the center of her chest to make sure she understands I'm serious.

She pulls her lips in, but stays put. I open the top drawer of my dresser and rummage around. *There it is.* A glass jar the color of jade. I pull it out with a grim smile.

"What's that?" Paige asks, her gaze curious but wary.

"Ointment. I got it in Hong Kong when I pulled a muscle."

"Let me guess. A stunt that you insisted on doing yourself?"

"Yup. And then they wouldn't let me do any of the other action sequences, so we had to have a stuntman come in. But this stuff is great. Got me back to normal in no time."

I open the jar and take out a dollop of the ointment on two fingers.

Paige wraps a hand around my wrist. "Is that stuff safe for pregnant women?"

"Yes."

She narrows her eyes. "How do you know?"

"Because it says so on the jar." I show her the label.

She takes her time reading it, but finally relaxes. "Okay."

The ointment is thick and gooey, but as I spread it over her flesh, it starts to thin. I massage it into her muscles. The key is making sure that it's fully absorbed. "I don't know what you think about me, Paige, but I'll never do anything to hurt you or your baby." *Even if you betray me.* I learned my lesson when I abandoned Lauren in Mexico. Even though I didn't mean for anything bad to happen, she still ended up dead because of my decision.

Paige leans forward until her forehead rests against mine. "Ryder…"

Her sweet breath fans against my skin. It tickles, but I welcome the sensation. When we're like this, it's like all the shit in the last forty-eight hours never happened.

I push away all the bitter memories and focus on Paige. Her eyes are closed, and she keeps dragging her teeth across her lower lip until it's red, wet and swollen.

My fingertips touch her lower belly. "You little rascal," I whisper. "You gave us quite a scare."

Her lashes are wet when she opens her eyes. When she breathes out my name again, it's like there's an invisible rope between us, and some unseen force is pulling me to her.

I dip my head and brush my mouth against hers. A small quiver flutters all along her skin.

I move my hand gently to her injured hip, giving it a little extra warmth, and deepen the kiss. Her lips part, and she brushes her tongue against mine tentatively. I sip at her sweet mouth, tracing her every curve, memorizing the shape and texture and fleshiness of her lips. A soft moan tears from her throat, and I press harder against her, making her swallow the sound.

Fire starts in my lions and spreads throughout my body. My blood sizzles as heat tightens my skin. I want her. And it's something beyond physical relief that I crave. I want her pleasure. I want her on her back, her legs spread, and screaming my name as I bury my cock deep inside her and pound into her over and over and over again, until she can't remember what it's like to be without my dick inside—

Suddenly, she lets out a sharp cry, and my eyes snap open immediately.

"That hurts."

My hand has tightened on her injured hip without my realizing. Cursing, I snatch it away.

What the hell was I thinking? Sex is the last thing she needs right now.

I stand up and shove my fingers into my hair. Having intercourse—or any kind of sex really—is probably the stupidest idea I could have had, given what happened earlier. I don't know anything about miscarriage risks, but I'm pretty sure inducing muscular contractions isn't on the list of recommended activities.

"Sorry," I say. "Bad idea."

"It's not your fault. We both got a little bit carried away."

"That doesn't mean it's okay. One of us needs to keep our cool."

She looks at me for a long time, then nods. "You're right. We should've kept our cool." She pulls her clothes up, wincing slightly as the hip bruise is covered again. She licks her lips, and her throat works. Her gaze darts from my face to her knee and back to my face.

The best thing to do would be to just take her to her room and end the evening now. But I know it's too late.

And then they come, those four dreaded words:

"We need to talk."

Paige

I can tell Ryder is looking for some graceful way to close the evening. But everything has just gotten to be too much. I can't pretend like everything is fine, head back to my room, shower and go to bed.

"Honestly, we should have talked in the morning when you first approached me," I add.

He merely looks at me, resting his hip against the dresser. Then he finally says, "Okay. Go ahead."

I lick my lips and voice the words I thought about during my drive back to his Beverly Hills mansion. "We should…" My throat closes up, and I can't say the next words. His taste still lingers on my lips, and I can still feel the imprint of his hand on my left hip. If I had a super power, I would go back in time and take Shaun's threat more seriously. But it's too late to wish for that now.

I drag in a deep breath and try again, because this is important. "We should quit now if you don't trust me. Given your history with Lauren, I don't think it would be good for you to be with a woman you suspect is using you for fame and fortune." I stop, suddenly uncertain. It sounded so much better in my head.

He's turned rigid. "It's only for a year."

The quiet, flat response tells me more than yelling and screaming would have. "Ryder. The biggest reason I was okay with this fake marriage was the fact that you trusted me. I thought I was doing it for my baby, but now I realize I wasn't."

"How did you come to that conclusion?"

"I thought about why I said okay. I could've found someone else who wouldn't have complicated my life the way you will."

He sighs but doesn't speak.

I forge on because this is important and he has to understand. "I can't be with a man who doesn't trust me. That's my minimum requirement. I don't expect love in an arrangement like this, but I deserve respect. And how can you have respect without trust?"

"You're right. You can't." He taps the edge of the dresser with a finger. "But shouldn't you earn that trust?"

"I think four years is plenty of time. And sometimes it's about a choice. You can choose to trust someone or not."

"A choice?" Ryder rolls the word, testing its shape and feel. "Kind of an odd thing to choose. Why should I make such a choice right now?"

"Because I'm not an actress. I can't convince people that I'm happy to be your bride when I know every time you look at me you see somebody who's using you. If we end it now, you still have time to find someone who can play the role to your liking."

Ryder doesn't answer me immediately. Instead the muscles in his jaw flex and twitch. Maybe he's taking the time to process what I'm telling him. After all, we only have three weeks until the ceremony. Or maybe he's angry that I want to end it. I'm pretty sure he's never thought that a woman would turn down a chance to be his wife. Most women would hack their way through half the Amazon jungle to get his ring on their finger.

I sigh and drop my gaze for a moment. "Anyway, you don't have to answer right now. I imagine you'll need some time to think it through and talk to your lawyers about the prenup and other arrangements you've already made. So… three days? Will that be enough?" I search his face, but I can't read him. He's completely closed off. "Just…let me know."

And with that, I get up and leave the room before I try to plead my case about the sex tape and how Shaun tried to use me. I've already said my piece on that subject. There's nothing more for me to do until Ryder makes his decision.

FOUR

Ryder

"Dude. What the hell are you doing here?" Elliot is staring at me like I'm insane. He told me he was at a strip club when I called to hang out. *A strip club*. But I decided to join him anyway, since there aren't that many people I can be with when I'm in this kind of mood. Now my half-brother spreads his hands like the world suddenly isn't making sense. "You're engaged."

I shrug. "Don't worry. I took the back entrance. Nobody saw me come in."

"That's not the point. You should be with Paige." Still, he moves over so I have enough space to park my ass on the couch next to him. He doesn't look like me, even though he's still handsome enough to turn heads from time to time. He got most of his looks from his mother. It's probably better that our father's genetics didn't express themselves. Dad's a top-tier asshole.

Elliot's in a dress shirt and slacks. I'm in a fresh button-down shirt and soft black denim pants.

He peers at me. "What happened to your face?"

I grimace. My lip still hurts. "There was a little incident."

"With what? A belligerent door?"

I snort. It's probably never crossed his mind that I would get into a fistfight. Violence isn't my thing. Way too much effort, for one. I can generally get what I want just by trading on looks and charm…and money and connections. Since I don't want to get into my morning confrontation with Anthony, I let my gaze roam the private room.

It's somewhere between swanky and gaudy. Three scantily dressed women move to the pounding beat on a hot pink stage, arching their backs and pelvises to accentuate their curves. Their small tops litter the shiny stage. Their feet, in clear platform hooker-heels, are spread apart, and their legs part lewdly, flashing thin strips of cloth nestling between their thighs. Since Elliot likes to splurge, we're in a VIP room alone with them. They all have a few hundred-dollar bills sticking out of their thongs, and there are two bottles of very good scotch on the table.

"Are you going to pick whoever collects the most benjamins from you?" I ask. Elliot needs to marry for the same reason I do, and he's sworn he's going to marry a stripper to spite our image-conscious father.

"Or…something." Elliot frowns. "Is everything okay? I saw the Tweets about your and Paige's visit to an ER."

"It's fine."

"The baby okay?"

Jesus. So the pregnancy won't be kept quiet until after the ceremony. "Yeah. No worries."

Elliot sits up straighter and gestures for the women to leave. They go, showering him with blown kisses and smoldering gazes intended to convey sexual heat. One of them looks like she's going to throw her back out swinging her hips as she walks away.

When we're alone, he asks, "Is it yours?"

"What do you think?"

"That you should go home and do the groom-to-be stuff."

I shake my head. "Paige wants to call it off."

"Whoa, for real? Why the hell would she want to do that?"

"She claims she can't go through with the whole thing if I don't trust her. Apparently, my questioning her about the sex tape means I'm the one doing something wrong."

"Did you let her know that you're willing to listen to her story? You were pretty upset."

"I never got a chance to say anything." Frankly, I didn't know *what* to say as soon as she opened her mouth and started talking about calling everything off. "She says I have to *choose* to believe her. Like that's how it works."

That's certainly no longer how it works with me. I chose to believe Lauren from the very beginning. And how did that work out? It ruined my friendship with Anthony and almost destroyed my relationship with Elliot. There's no question that the four-year history between me and Paige has erected a large edifice of trust. But what she did took a wrecking ball to the foundation. If her ex was really continuing to harass her, she should've told me. I would've taken care of it. She knows I have an entire team at my disposal to deal with annoying assholes.

But she didn't. Is someone in my position supposed to take everything people say at face value, especially when things go south? And the whole "sex tape being released on the night of our engagement party" drove everything so fucking south, it ran smack into Antarctica.

Elliot pours me some scotch. "Well... If you want to back out, now's the time. Mira and Christopher can spin it so that you won't come out of the whole thing looking like some kind of an asshole. I mean, people are going to understand why you wouldn't want to marry a woman who was caught screwing someone else on video."

I knock back the drink and scowl at the heat singeing my throat. It isn't that simple, and he doesn't get it. But then how could he? I don't even know why I feel the way I do. It's not the first time a woman has stabbed me in the back.

Lauren's betrayal infuriated me as much as it gutted me. Even as I tried to deny all the signs and evidence, my brain working overtime to come up with one implausible explanation after another for her behavior, my heart told me I was deluding myself. But with Paige, it's different. I want to ignore the evidence and just accept her explanation that she's a victim and that she honestly has zero interest in fame. Certainly she's never indicated that she wanted to be in the business when she was working for me as my assistant. But Mira's also right: people can change. Lauren didn't do drugs when we first met either.

"I'm sorry I recommended Paige," Elliot says, rubbing his forehead. "I honestly thought she would be good for you. Maybe you should follow your instincts and do it with some new model or actress whose agenda is clear. That way nothing they do can surprise you."

I raise a hand to block his apology. "Not your fault. I'm the one who made the final decision."

I take a long swallow of the scotch. My feelings are all jumbled. I feel like someone who was lost at sea and got tantalizingly close to reaching land, only to be carried away by the tides. But when I think about my grandfather's portrait, I'm just…numb. And empty.

What is Paige going to do when she's free of me? Ending our engagement won't change the fact that she's pregnant. And of course she'll want the child taken care of. And that will require money…

Something's been niggling at my mind, and it won't go away. I try to relax, let the thought come…

The jacket. The one Paige was wearing knotted around her waist to cover up the blood-stain on her skirt.

It was a man's jacket.

I pull out my phone and call the house. The housekeeper answers.

"Sue, there's a man's jacket in Paige's laundry. Black, and too large for her. Can you check and tell me if the buttons have any particular letter or anything on them?"

"Hold on a sec." A few minutes pass by, then

she returns to the line. "Okay, I'm looking at it. Yes. They all have this big capital 'R.'"

"Done like calligraphy, with the tail of the R in a kind of curlicue?"

"Uh huh. Like something out of a bible."

I thank her and hang up.

Dad.

He doesn't wear anything that cheap, but his chauffeur Perry does. Dad likes to have Rs on the staff uniforms. It makes him feel special, like he's some kind of fucking royalty.

Paige avoided talking about who gave her a ride from the hospital. If it was no big deal, she would've told me. But she knows how things are between me and my father.

It is absolutely conceivable that Dad told her to do this. It's not like he's unable to offer her money. For I know, she could've released the sex tape herself because that's what Dad wanted in return for some astounding sum.

Damn. This is so fucked up.

Even though Paige downplayed the money stuff in Samantha's office, she could have had second thoughts. Or just gotten greedy. Buyers' remorse is more common than people think. Just because they don't tell you that they changed their mind out of fear of looking unreliable doesn't mean they aren't going to let their greed guide them.

I find that I'm breathing through my mouth. The scotch sits like acid in my belly, and my gut twists. Less than forty hours ago, I felt like the king of the world. I had a proper fiancée by my side, and my grandfather's portrait was soon to be mine. Now everything feels ashen and dull.

Elliot gives me more scotch, then helps himself to some as well. "If you're going to marry Paige in spite of everything, you two should present a united front. Unless you want to have people talking about your marriage forever."

I grimace. He's right, but I don't want to discuss this crap anymore. "Bring the girls back in. I know you're shopping for a bride."

An easy grin pops on his face. "Don't know if I want those same three. I'm not really seeing anybody my type."

"Do you actually have a type?"

"Of course! Big tits and a nice ass, something to hold onto when I fuck her."

I laugh in spite of myself. Good old Elliot. Never serious about women, and there's something in his gaze that looks almost pained every time he thinks of marriage.

And why shouldn't he feel awful? Marriage is a terrible thing. Just look at how it's complicating my life, and I haven't even exchanged vows with my fiancée yet.

I close my eyes and imagine what the ceremony is going to be like. But no matter how I try, I can't picture anybody except Paige next to me.

Perhaps I should just go ahead. Like I told her, it's only for a year, and it won't be that hard to create a united front. I can start the process by ruining the son of a bitch who released that sex tape.

"Gotta go," I say. "Good luck bride hunting."

As I make my way downstairs, a topless woman is coming up. She pushes her tits my way. She's a bottle blonde with dark roots showing. Her boobs are so plastic, she literally bounces back when she bumps me with them. "Where you going? You just got here." She gives me an overly happy smile. "If you can wait just a few minutes, I'll get off. And then *we* can go and get off."

Despite all the artifice, she's a good-looking woman. And if I'd run into her a month ago, maybe I would've said yes. But now I'm just not interested. She doesn't have the softness or the natural curves that heat my blood.

And that's another reason things seem hopeless. I can't even interest myself in other women. I don't know if it's the promise I made Paige about being faithful so long as we're together—I've never broken a promise to anyone—or something else…but a part of me broods in bitterness as I drive home.

FIVE

Paige

I SHOULD PROBABLY GO TO BED AND GET SOME rest, but I can't seem to get my brain to cut off. I sit up after a while and make my way downstairs. Simon and Mom are leaving for Sweet Hope tomorrow. Instead of stewing in bed, I should spend some time with them. Mom is a night owl after all.

My hip is better as I walk to the guest-house where Simon and Mom are staying. Ryder's magic ointment seems to be working.

As I walk through the massive garden, I can't help but feel a slight bit of regret that I ended up ruining what could've been a nice moment. I know I did the right thing by airing out what's been festering between us, but the part of me that prefers to bury my head in the sand would've been happier if we'd just made out and faked everything.

After all, our current relationship is fake. What's one more bit of fakery on top of a towering cake of fakeness?

I ring the door at the guest-house. The light is on in the main living room. Despite the unpretentious name, the place is a mini-mansion with multiple suites and a full-time housekeeper. The door opens and reveals my mom in a housedress with a pink and yellow flower design. "Paige! I didn't know you were still up."

"Couldn't fall asleep. Is Simon up too?"

She shakes her head. "Dead to the world. He was wiped out from sightseeing today. Ryder's people did a great job of setting everything up so it wasn't overly tiring, and we got to see a lot of what we've always wanted to see. But you know how Simon is. Doesn't do well without his routines."

I grin. Simon is such an influence in my life, but sometimes he reminds me of a child.

"And you?" She searches my face. "Are you all right?"

"Yeah, sure. Fine."

She frowns. I don't think she buys that at all. But then I guess that's what makes her a mother. "Want to take a walk?" she asks.

"Aren't you tired?"

"Oh, I can manage a midnight stroll. I'm younger than your father after all."

That makes me chuckle. "Okay. Let's go."

She puts a hand in the crook of my arm. The garden is dark except for lamps set in elaborate knee-high wrought iron posts. We walk side-by-side on the pebbled path that winds through rose bushes and other flowering plants I don't know the name of.

"This is a gorgeous garden. And so functional, too."

"Functional?"

"There's a vegetable patch in the back. I also saw some herbs and berries."

"Oh."

"You never noticed?"

I shake my head. "No. I've seen some of his garden, but never really explored the entire place here."

We reach the man-made pond. The surface is covered with water lilies, and always reminds me of Monet. We sit on a bench, listening to the chirping of the night bugs.

"How are you holding up?" Mom asks.

"Great," I say, trying for offhand cheer.

She gives me a stern, penetrating look, the kind that seems to peer into your soul.

"All right. Not great. It's been hard."

She takes my hand and pats it as if to say "there there."

"That damn tape has just…made a mess of everything. And I'm really sorry. I know it's affecting you as well."

"Sometimes people betray our trust, but that doesn't mean it's your fault."

Don't I know it? But knowing intellectually and knowing something deep in your heart are two different things. I stare at the lilies, silvery black in the moonlight. "I wish Dad were alive."

Mom's hand tightens around mine. "What do you mean?" Her voice is brittle, and the words sound forced. It's like she'd rather talk about anything but Dad.

No real surprise, once I stop to think about it. I haven't talked about Dad in forever.

"It's just…" I turn fully toward her. "If Dad were alive, I might not feel the need to be perfect all the time."

Even in the dim light, I can see Mom's face crumple. The lines around her eyes seem to deepen, and her lips thin.

I must've stunned her. Despite thinking about him from time to time, I don't talk about him because I don't want to pain Mom. The stories she's told me about him are lovely, and I know if he'd lived, he would've been Father of the Century.

Leaning closer, Mom lowers her voice. "Has Simon ever told you you were disappointing in some—?"

"No!" I say quickly before she jumps to any conclusions. "Simon's always been great. But I do worry about disappointing him. I always feel like the good things we have in our life might disappear unless I'm good."

Mom gasps. "Paige, my dear." She puts her arms around me. "We'll love you no matter what. Sometimes bad things happen to good people, and it's not because they made a mistake or because they weren't perfect."

"You know I'm pregnant."

Mom pulls back. "Is that the reason for this sudden marriage?"

Well, there's more to it than that. But I don't want to get into all the details. "Basically."

"I see." Mom holds both my hands in hers, warming them. My mother's hands aren't the softest, but they're very comforting. "You shouldn't feel obligated to make a decision—one that can impact your life so much—just because of the baby. Simon and I can help you with it if need be. And if you don't feel like that's an option, well, there's always abortion."

My entire body stills. A hard ball lodges in my chest. "What? But…it's your grandchild."

"I know, but... Honestly, it's better not to have a child if it's unwanted." Mom straightens her spine, pulling her shoulders back. "Marriage can have serious repercussions. When you marry somebody like Ryder, the effects are amplified. Don't let one unintended pregnancy decide the rest of your life. You're still so young. A responsibility as big as a child closes a lot of doors."

I sit there in stunned silence, trying to process what she's telling me. Mom isn't saying anything outrageous. But the thought of terminating the pregnancy never occurred to me. And even now, the idea is just...alien.

"Don't look at me like that, Paige. I'm not telling you to get rid of the baby. I'm telling you to consider all your options before making a decision. I don't want to see you in pain. And frankly, I'm not sure if Ryder is the right man to make you happy. We're just too different."

"Obviously. He's a big movie star."

Mom shakes her head. "Even if he weren't a movie star, we would still be too different. You saw how his parents were. When you marry someone, you're marrying their family too." There is an odd tension—and maybe a little fear? —in her gaze as she looks at me. "I've done everything I could to ensure that you have a good life. Your happiness is all that matters to me."

Unable to speak, I nod.

She yawns. "Now, I should probably get some sleep. We have an early flight home tomorrow."

"Ryder's jet is very comfortable," I say.

"I know. But I can't sleep on planes."

We walk back to the guest-house. I give her a tight hug and make my way back to my suite.

I open the small drawer in my vanity. Inside are a few grainy ultrasound prints. They show dates and a tiny—but growing—dot.

I run my finger over the sesame seed-sized cluster of cells that is my baby. It has complicated my life so much already. Not to mention, it is half Shaun, who is doing his best to ruin everything. But I can't hate the baby. In spite of all that, the idea of losing it makes my chest hurt.

I'm hopelessly in love with the life growing in my womb. And I know I'm going to do everything in my power to protect it.

SIX

Ryder

Something wakes me up.

I would've preferred some extra sleep. My head feels like there's a platoon of Marines marching through it...all of them with jackhammers.

I flip onto my back, trying for some extra Zs, and wince. The pajamas I have on are constricting. I don't even know who put me in them. I usually sleep in my boxer sh—

Raising my head, I look down at myself and curse. I'm not in pajamas, I'm still in the clothes I put on to go to the club. My head drops back on the pillow. I don't need to consciously sniff to know that I stink.

Of course I know why I'm in this condition. It's all that drinking and thinking about Paige's ultimatum. I hate being cornered into making a decision. And despite what Elliot said, it's not about what I want. No. It's all about Paige's threat.

I look at the bedside clock. *Almost noon.* There's something I have to do... But what the hell was it?

I jackknife up, and pain explodes like a bomb in my head. I put the heels of both hands to my temples. Maggie and Simon are supposed to fly home this morning, and I was planning to go to the airport with them. But since I overslept, they probably left without me.

Gritting my teeth, I struggle up, swallow four aspirins, and drag myself into the shower. Getting out of my clothes is so difficult I seriously consider just walking into the stall with them on. But eventually I'm nude and under the hot and cleansing water. It feels like heaven, and the temptation to linger is overwhelming. But, stuff to do. I change into a clean t-shirt and shorts and walk barefoot to the kitchen to get some coffee.

Elizabeth and Paige are at the counter, their golden heads close like a couple of conspirators. My sister is wearing a pink sheath dress, while Paige is in sweats. They're laughing over something, and Elizabeth rests her fingertips on the rim of a black mug that says *Sexiest Man Alive*. As irritated as I am, it warms my heart to see Paige happy. It's almost like yesterday never happened. I note with approval that she remains seated at the counter when Elizabeth gets up to put away the tea and cookies they were having.

"Morning, sleepy-head," Elizabeth says, tossing her curls over a shoulder. "Or maybe it's more like good afternoon."

"I would've gotten up earlier if somebody had woken me."

Paige's expression goes neutral. "The housekeeper said that you came home late, so I didn't want to bother you."

I hate it that I'm the reason the merry spark vanishes from her eyes and the fact that it's making me feel like the villain here. My mood takes an ugly dive.

"Coffee?" Elizabeth asks, a determined smile on her lips. She isn't going to let the tension between me and Paige ruin everything.

"Thanks." I rub my temples. "Where's the chef?"

"Taking a break. I think we can fend for ourselves for one meal," my sister says. "But if you want something fancy…"

I wave it away. "Forget it. I can't stomach anything other than coffee right now." Once I feel better, I'll have a smoothie or something. But I don't need the chef for that.

Soon, Elizabeth places the coffee in front of me in a mug that reads *The Person Drinking Out of This Is an Ugly Ogre*, a gag gift from her two Christmases ago. I start chugging it down. As the hot brew settles in my gut, I start to feel almost human again.

The doorbell rings, and a few minutes later, my housekeeper Sue walks in with a huge bouquet of blue hyacinths and white tulips.

"Who are they for?" I ask.

Sue looks mildly apologetic. "The delivery guy didn't say."

"Ah, one of Elizabeth's secret admirers." Even though she discourages them, she has her share of men who won't accept no for an answer. They're mostly harmless, albeit a little slow on the uptake.

"Doubt that," she says with a soft snort, but her eyes say otherwise.

"Regardless, they're beautiful," Paige says.

"They are. At least whoever sent them has good taste." Elizabeth takes the flowers, pulls the card and reads it. "Dear Paige. Sorry about yesterday and I do hope you feel better." She pauses for a moment. "Anthony."

My coffee mug hits the counter with a loud thunk. "What the fuck?"

My sister clears her throat and hands the bouquet to Paige. I wait for her to toss it on the ground. Flowers from Anthony aren't fit to be turned into compost for my garden.

Instead, she puts them close to her face and inhales. "They smell nice."

Elizabeth lowers her head for a sniff. "Wow. They really do."

"Guess I'll put them in my room."

I almost spew my coffee. Anthony's flowers in my fiancée's room? In *my home?* I don't think so.

But apparently Paige is serious. Holding the big bouquet like it's a baby, she walks out. A moment later I hear her going up the stairs.

I start to get up, but Elizabeth puts a hand on my forearm. "Let it go. Paige can deal with the problem. Don't you trust her?"

"It's not Paige. It's Anthony I don't trust."

"At least finish your coffee before you go." Elizabeth lowers her voice. "Do you honestly think people don't know what you were up to last night?"

"What?"

"You went to a strip club with Elliot." Her lips purse in disapproval. "Not the smartest move."

I curse under my breath. "How did you know?"

"Photos? Elliot going in first, then you following him in later? Everyone has a camera on their phone. Your privacy isn't safe no matter where you go, especially in this town. You're just too high profile."

Shit. I thought I'd gotten away with it. "Think Paige knows?"

"I don't think so. She hasn't said or done anything. But you have to be more careful."

"Nothing happened. I swear. You can ask Elliot."

"It isn't about what happened or didn't happen. It's the perception."

Of course. I rub my face. Everything is always about perception.

I gulp down my coffee as quickly as possible. I don't want to fight with Paige, but I'm not going to be weak and run away when she's obviously spoiling for one. I can't think of any other reason for her to want to keep Anthony's bouquet.

After placing the empty mug on the counter with more force than necessary, I run upstairs to find Paige. She's in her room, and I see the offending flowers in a crystal vase on the bedside table.

I grind my teeth at the sight. Bad enough that she has Anthony's flowers in her room, but right next to her bed?

Elizabeth's warning echoes in my head. So I try for some calm. "I'd appreciate it if you threw those out."

Paige tilts her head. "Is that your answer to what I said yesterday?"

"No." I grind my teeth. "Actually, maybe. If you want me to trust you, then act in ways that inspire my trust."

"How should I act?"

"Not associating with people who want to hurt me would be a start. And for god's sake, don't keep stuff sent by them."

She raises her chin. "That's all it'll take for you to trust me?"

The defiance in her gaze rubs me raw. "Not quite." I never give a definite answer to anything. "But close."

"Right. So even if I do everything perfectly, there still won't be any trust." She looks at me with a coldness I'm not accustomed to seeing from her. "What you want is control. You want to decide who I see, who I can associate with, who I talk to. There's nothing equal about that sort of relationship."

The accusation pisses me off. I've never done anything to control her. She's the one who decided to push my buttons by bringing Anthony's flowers to her room, knowing how I feel about him. Knowing what happened between the two of us. "I've never treated you any different from before, so you being upset like this all of a sudden is bullshit, and you know it. If you want my attention, fine. Get it in a more productive way, not like this."

She pales. "You think it's all about attention?"

"What else could it be?" I really can't imagine. "Payback because I invited your folks over without your permission?"

Breaking eye contact, she paces back and forth twice, then stops. Her gaze comes back to me, and this time there's hot fury in it. "The fact that you don't treat me any different is the problem. You want me to be your wife, *allegedly*, but you're still treating me like I'm your assistant."

I open my mouth to refute her. She's being emo—

"*I'm not finished.*" Her hands are on her hips and her chest rises and falls. "My situation now is worse than when I was your assistant, because you never cared who sent me flowers before. Now I can't even seem to breathe without your permission."

"That's unfair!" I always hated it when she got flowers from some guy she was seeing. I just never showed it because how can you do that without looking like a psycho? She'd always giggle and flush with pleasure, and weirdly enough, I hated seeing her like that over some stuff that some guy sent her.

"Oh, so I *can* breathe without your say-so? Great! Then they"—she gestures at the flowers—"stay because I like them. Now if you'll excuse me, I need to clear my head."

She stalks out without waiting for my response. I glare at the damned bouquet. If that's how it's going to be, fine. But she should know she isn't the only one who can draw a line in the sand.

Paige

I GO OUT FOR A WALK. IT'S EITHER THAT OR scream at Ryder.

After I make a huge circle around the rose garden, my temper starts to cool. I've been asking Ryder to make the decision to trust me. Perhaps it's about time I make that easier for him. Given his history with Anthony, my keeping the flowers probably doesn't help. Besides, there's the whole blowup Ryder had over the interview I scheduled with Derek Madison from *The Hollywood News*.

A part of me wants to have that interview more than ever before. It would be a chance to tell my side of the story, especially after the sex tape. But given Ryder's history with Lauren, I can see how the whole situation looks to him. I should cancel.

And when I get back, I should throw out the flowers…even though they *are* really pretty.

Ryder isn't the enemy. Yes, his reaction to the tape and so on hurt. A lot. But his concern for me and my baby's welfare is genuine. I shouldn't ignore that and only look at the bad parts.

I sit on the same bench that I shared with Mom last night. The lake is calm, the lily leaves like enormous green coins in the water.

My hand goes to my belly of its own volition. Mom told me to get rid of the baby if it makes sense, but I can't. Even now I feel a deep bonding with my child.

I pull out my phone and call Derek. He answers within seconds, like he's been waiting for me. "Paige. How are you?"

"Good, tha—"

"I saw the news. You're out of danger, right?"

Oh, lord. "I'm fine, thanks. Did, um…everyone see it?"

"Everyone with social media, I imagine."

I shake my head. "I'm just not used to this."

"Better *get* used to it. You're a big star. Everyone wants to know about you now."

But not the truth. All they want to know is the dirt, not the real me. "I'm calling you about that exclusive we were planning."

"Uh oh, that doesn't sound good."

"Yeah, I'm really sorry. But I don't think I can do it anymore. It… It doesn't feel right."

"I see." He pauses, then clears his throat. "I don't know how to say this delicately, but is it because the wedding's off?"

I have to laugh. "You're fishing. Even if it were, you know I couldn't tell you anything definite right now."

"Really?" The word is laden with skepticism. "I ask because there've been some reports that Ryder was seen at a strip club last night with his brother."

All the air gushes out of my lungs, and I grip my phone tightly. That must've been after our dinner. And the brother must've been Elliot. Blake and Lucas don't indulge Ryder the same way. But despite his image, Elliot can be surprisingly sensible. I can't imagine him dragging Ryder to a strip club. And why would Ryder go to one after our talk about trust? "Those reports must be mistaken," I say. "Ryder was home last night." Then I add, "With me."

Why am I lying like this? Maybe I don't want to look any more pathetic than I already do. But my stomach is churning, and what little I have in it wants to come up. I clench my teeth.

"Huh. Must've been an error, then," Derek says. He sniffs. "Well, I'm disappointed about not getting that interview. Not gonna lie. But I'm happy for you that the wedding's going to happen as planned. Calling it off now would look bad, especially for the bride."

"Of course," I rasp.

"Maybe in another month or two?"

I nod, then remember that I'm on the phone. "Yeah. Sure."

I hang up and shove the phone back into my pocket. When Ryder came home drunk last night, I assumed he went out drinking with Elliot to blow off steam. The notion that he went someplace racier than your average bar never crossed my mind. The core issue between us has been his inability to trust that I'm not like Lauren. I trusted that he would keep his word to me—that he wouldn't do anything to humiliate me. I guess my trust was misplaced, or else he has an odd definition of "humiliation."

Unable to sit still, I walk home. My mind churns with thoughts, and my heart is full of conflicting emotions. But I have to talk to Ryder now. I don't think I can function without that first.

When I walk in, Sue is coming downstairs with a black trash bag. "Are you all right?" she asks. "You look a little flushed."

"I'm fine," I say quickly. I must look horrible for her to remark on it. But then she usually sees me all made up and everything. "Have you seen Ryder?"

"He just went to his office."

"Thanks." I walk up to the second floor.

His office is past the assistant's—the one I used to work out of until a few days ago.

Ryder's workspace isn't exactly "corporate". It's a big area with lots of comfortable loungers and low tables that he can place drinks on. Instead of books, he has photos of places he's been on built-in shelves. There's also a fascinating bit of art on one wall: a nearly empty canvas with just a few black lines and lots of white space, done by a Korean artist. He paid some insane amount of money for it at an auction, calling it "beautiful emptiness." I'm not sure if that's actually the title of the piece or not.

He's on a barcalounger, drinking another coffee. A stack of paper rests on his lap, and from the looks of it, he's perusing another script. He glances my way. "Thought you went out for a walk."

I close the door behind me. "I'm done now." I take a love seat and cross my legs.

Setting aside the script, he sits up straight. His eyes are guarded. "You okay?"

"Is it true you went to a strip club with Elliot?"

Something flickers in his gaze, then he frowns. "Who told you that?"

"Does it matter?"

"Probably not." He sighs. "Yes. Well, technically, I didn't go *with* him. I met him at one because he was there and didn't want to go anywhere else."

"Am I supposed to believe that?"

"Of course you're supposed to believe it. You think I'm lying?"

He's meeting my gaze straight on. Normally I'd think the person was telling the truth. But this is Ryder, one of the best actors around.

"Look, Paige. I don't care what you heard, but nothing happened. And you know I'd never talk about private stuff in front of a bunch of strippers."

"How do I know you went there to talk?"

A dull red rises in his cheeks. "Are you telling me you don't trust me? Especially after that stuff about how trust is more a decision than anything?"

A fist lodges in my throat, and I can barely breathe. It takes a moment before I can gather my thoughts enough to speak. "This isn't about tit-for-tat, Ryder."

"I never said it was. You're the one who's grilling me here over some gossip. You know how it is in Hollywood. Everyone puts the absolute worst spin on everything."

It pains me that he doesn't see how that's true of me too, because of my association with him. But it's obvious that he thinks I'm some kind of exception.

And the truth is I'm pretty certain he's right. He can't even smile at another woman without it becoming a big deal. But the fact that he won't give me the same benefit of the doubt he's asking for hurts. I can't decide if I should scream or cry.

"Paige…"

I jump to my feet. "I can't continue right now."

Before he can stop me, I go to my room. I need to be somewhere quiet to process all this so I don't do anything rash.

But when I open the door to my suite, a white-hot rage sears my entire body, leaving my skin raw and tight. For a moment I can't think or even breathe. Then all the emotion gathers in my belly like a knot of angry snakes.

Gone are the blue hyacinths and white tulips. Instead, there are red, yellow and purple tulips in a different crystal vase on my bedside table.

The bouquet is just as large and beautiful as the one from Anthony. It probably cost just as much, if not more.

Ryder follows me in. Concern softens his voice. "Paige, look—"

"Did you do this?" I ask, my jaw tight.

"What?"

I gesture at the tulips. "Where are the hyacinths?"

Tense lines form on his forehead. "The housekeeper knocked the vase over when she came up here to clean your room."

The fury in my gut explodes. "*Am I supposed to believe such a lame excuse?*" Something close to hysteria edges my voice, raising it until it's shrill.

"Oh, for fuck's sake! Now what? Is there going to be another inquisition over some flowers?" His expression is no longer placid or concerned. It is one of pure justified outrage.

"If you'd just waited, I would've thrown them out myself. I decided to do that when I was out walking. But no—you had to take care of it yourself, didn't you? You weren't going to let me decide." I reach into the closet and pull out a small suitcase. I open it and start tossing in some essentials—underwear, moisturizer and some changes of clothes.

"What the hell are you doing?"

"Can't you tell?"

The sound of his breathing rings harshly in the room. He rakes his hair, then glares at me. "Dammit, Paige. If you walk out now, it's over."

I zip the bag. Suddenly I'm drained and empty. Tears prickle at my eyes, but I hold them back. They won't do a thing to fix the situation.

"No, Ryder," I tell him, facing him with my hand around the suitcase handle. "It was over when you decided that I was the one who released the sex tape for fame and fortune."

SEVEN

Paige

It takes me over an hour to reach my stepsister's house. The traffic is atrocious, even for Los Angeles, and makes me contemplate moving to a mountain top somewhere in the Himalayas.

I ring the bell and wait. Bethany and Oliver have given me free run of the place, but I don't like to walk in unannounced since they're still rather passionate about each other. After a few moments the door opens wide and Bethany steps out. She's in a bright sunflower-yellow t-shirt and faded denim capris. A yellow number two pencil skewers a messy brown bun on top of her head. It's her "I'm home and comfy" look.

She notes my suitcase, and a concerned expression comes over her face. Instead of asking questions, she pulls me inside.

I walk into the homey living room. Oliver adjusts his glasses as he walks out of the kitchen. His gaze drops to the suitcase, and a frown appears. "What's going on?"

I stand by the couch, shifting my weight from one foot to the other. "I know it's sudden, but I need a place to stay for a while. Normally I'd go back to my apartment, but there are too many reporters."

Bethany and Oliver exchange a quick look. She takes charge. After all, I'm her family. "Of course, you're welcome to stay with us as long as you need. But… I thought you were getting married."

"In less than three weeks. Is Ryder calling things off?" Disapproval pinches Oliver's face.

"Not exactly," I say. "But I guess they're off now." Ryder made that clear when he issued his ultimatum.

The silence in the room seems to suck all the air out, waiting and anticipating. I resist the urge to babble. The entire mess is just too embarrassing to share with my brother-in-law, even though he's a sweetheart and I adore him.

Bethany comes over and hugs me tightly. "I'm so sorry, honey."

Oliver pats my shoulder awkwardly. "Yeah, um… If you guys would like to talk privately…"

I shake my head. "It's all right."

Bethany puts a hand at the small of my back and leads me upstairs. "Let me show you to your room."

They have three bedrooms. The biggest one is the master bedroom, and the smallest is a home office where Bethany does most of her web comic work. The medium-sized one is for overnight guests and has a double bed. Pale green sheets with an ivy pattern cover the mattress. The curtains are cool mint green against the light cream wall. Even though the room isn't that large, it feels somewhat spacious because of the colors.

I set the suitcase at the foot of the bed and perch on the edge of the mattress. My knees shake, and fatigue settles all the way to my bones.

"Are you really all right?" Bethany asks, settling next to me.

"I'm fine. Just a little tired. I didn't sleep well last night."

"Not surprising. I saw the news. The baby, right?"

I nod. We didn't talk about anything like that when we accompanied Mom and Simon to the airport, but Bethany would have to be deaf and blind not to hear about it.

"I wish you'd told me," she says.

Blinking away the tears before she can notice them, I put my elbows on my knees and clasp my hands together. "I'd just found out when you made your announcement. I didn't want to steal your thunder."

"Oh, Paige. You know it's not like that."

"I know. But at the time I wasn't sure what I was going to do, or what was going to happen… If I was going to be a single mom or…what. I didn't want to say anything until I knew for certain."

She sighs. "Ryder should do the right thing. It's his baby, too."

I press my lips together. I can't tell Bethany what's really going on. It's not that I don't trust her to be discreet. It's just that I can't let anybody know the entire truth behind the deal Ryder and I struck. Even if he made it clear what he thinks of me, I don't want to be petty just to get back at him. Undoubtedly he'll move on—there are thousands of eager women for him. It won't take him long to find a woman who can play the role he wants.

Bethany squeezes my hand. "I'm glad you decided to crash at our place. There are pictures of us at the airport with Mom and Dad. It looks like everyone's tracking your movements."

The idea that people are watching me like that makes my skin crawl. I saw how bad it was for Ryder, but it's one thing to watch it happen to someone else and another to experience it firsthand. "I'm really sorry. I'll find a place soon. I don't want you to lose your privacy because of me."

She snorts. "Don't even think about it. They're welcome to watch me drive to the grocery store, the post office…and my gynecologist! I'm so boring, they'll lose interest within a week." She puts an arm around my shoulder. "No matter what, you have me and Oliver. And Mom and Dad, too. We love you and we won't let anything happen to you, okay? So cheer up. I want to see you smile."

Her unconditional love thaws the cold knot in my chest, and I manage a tiny smile.

"There you go." She tightens her hold on me. "Have you had dinner yet? If not, Oliver made a killer quesadilla and guacamole…unless you can't keep anything down?"

I shake my head. "No morning sickness. And I'm ravenous. I'll join you."

"We already ate, but I'll set you a place and re-heat some of the food. Come on down whenever you're ready."

The wooden stairs creak under her steps. I inhale the mild detergent on the sheets and will myself to cheer up. Moping won't solve anything, and I have to pull myself together. I'm going to need a new job and a place to stay ASAP.

But first things first. It's time to eat and fortify myself. I won't waste away like some distraught

Victorian maid. Paige Johnson is made of sterner stuff.

So I get up and pull myself together. When I reach the dining room, one end of the rectangular table has a plate piled with quesadillas, a bowl of what looks like homemade guacamole and some salsa. At the other end is a stack of papers. Bethany is reading through them, a frown on her face.

Oliver hands me a glass of OJ, and I take my seat. His quesadillas are amazing, gooey with tons of cheese. I eat in silence for a few minutes, just savoring the food.

Finally, the edge comes off my hunger. "What's that?" I gesture at the papers.

"The contract for that investment," Bethany answers without looking up. She jots something down in a spiral notebook. "My web comic thing."

"Any problems?" I ask. Her brows are pinched with more than just concentration.

"It's just so…grabby. It's like nothing I create would be my own anymore. Ditto for the other artists I want to showcase. I can't have that. I need to talk to my lawyer about it." She purses her mouth.

"Can't you just walk away? You can just raise the capital you need through crowd funding."

She shakes her head. "It isn't that simple. I'll owe them fifty thousand dollars in a break-up fee."

My jaw slackens. "Oh my gosh."

"It's my fault. I should've read the initial agreement more carefully. I was so excited that I basically skimmed it."

Oliver squeezes her shoulder. "It's not your fault. Anybody in your position would've done the same."

I nod. "What your wise husband said. I'm sure you'll find a way to make it work. You're too smart not to."

"Thanks," Bethany says. Her chin firms a bit. "And you're right. I will." She returns to the contract.

I munch on the food, watching my stepsister. No matter what she faces, I know she'll find a way through. She's the kind of person I've always wanted to be…but somehow can't seem to manage to become.

EIGHT

Paige

THE NEXT DAY, THE HOUSE IS EMPTY AFTER breakfast. Oliver went to work, and Bethany went to see her lawyer.

I sit on the IKEA couch and tap my knees. Not having anything to do feels *really* weird. Normally, I'm on call even on weekends and have errands to run on Ryder's behalf. Once we got engaged, I spent most of my time being dragged around by his personal shopper and fashion consultant. To have an entire day when I don't have to be anywhere or deal with anybody? It feels like I stepped through a portal into some alternate universe.

A dark remote on the coffee table catches my attention. I start to flip through the channels, then stop when a show mentions me and Ryder.

The well-dressed hosts with perfect makeup and perfect hair and perfectly bleached teeth talk about us like we're some kind of gossip topic. I guess we are, except I've never been in this kind of situation before.

They speculate about why Ryder is marrying me—probably the baby, and they talk about why I should be careful because things like that surely can't last even if the man in question *is* known for donating huge sums of money to help underprivileged women and children.

"I mean, there's a big difference between donating once in a while and dealing with it yourself every day for the next eighteen years," says a blue-eyed blonde who looks positively gleeful.

"At least it solves the mystery of why he's marrying her," a brunette says. "It was on a lot of people's minds."

Bitch.
Fat cow.
Beached whale.

And so many other hateful things said about me online flood my mind. My hands start shaking, and I turn the TV off. I don't need the stress.

The doorbell rings. Grateful for something to do, I get up. It's probably a delivery man, but I check through the peephole anyway.

Standing outside is Elliot Reed. I open the door.

He's in a white t-shirt and denim shorts, his feet stuck in black flip-flops. A pair of sunglasses dangles from one hand.

Despite the fact that he's Ryder's half-brother, they look nothing alike. I heard that he takes after his mother, who was Wife Number Two. His hair is dark, but compared to Ryder's it's a shade or two lighter. He also didn't get the classic Pryce profile with those perfect, aristocratic lines. But he's still a striking man, with even features and a charming smile.

Unfortunately for him, I'm immune.

"What are you doing here?" I ask.

He gives me the smile. "I happened to be in the neighborhood."

"Right. Because you routinely hang out in middle class neighborhoods that don't have high-end bars or strip clubs."

"Ouch," he says with a wince. "Guess I deserved that."

I give him a look.

"Can I come in?"

"If Ryder sent you—"

"He didn't."

I gaze at him, wondering. "All right," I say finally. "You can come in."

He walks in, looking around the humble living room. It's smaller than Ryder's bedroom, and it is decorated with inexpensive furniture and second-hand items. Shelves have tons of framed pictures of Oliver and Bethany—an unbroken photographic record from the time they became an item to the present.

"Nice," he murmurs.

"I bet you've never set foot in a house that's worth less than three million."

Something flashes in his gaze, then disappears just as quickly as it appeared. "Now who's being a snob?" He sits in the couch. "Elizabeth called me."

I frown. "About?"

"You."

Crossing my arms, I lean against the wall across from him. "If there's anything she wants to talk to me about, she knows my number."

"Yeah, well. I thought I should do this face-to-face."

I keep my mouth shut and wait for him to go on.

"Nothing happened at the strip club," he says.

My lips curve. "Riiiiiight."

"Look, Ryder wanted to talk, I was already there, and I didn't want to leave. So he came by."

"Regular bars not good enough for you guys?" I say, uncrossing my arms.

"You know about the deal with our father, don't you?"

I nod. No point in being coy with him.

"I thought so." He taps his lips like I've just confirmed something important for him. "Then you know I need to marry too."

"And how does that relate to the strip club?"

He frowns and smiles at the same time, like you do when someone doesn't get an obvious joke. "I'm looking for a wife."

My mouth opens, but nothing comes out. His announcement has short-circuited my brain.

Now he actually laughs. "You haven't heard?"

"No." I blink. "But why? You could have anybody you want."

"Maybe that's exactly why I want a stripper. Besides, it'll be more fun this way. You watch." He winks.

Then it hits me. Why he's doing this—it's to show to his father that he can't be controlled. I snort a laugh. "You are *terrible*."

"Thank you. I try very hard." He grows serious. "Paige, why are you making this more complicated than it needs to be?"

I sigh, then shake my head. "Ryder doesn't trust me."

"And? So what? It's only for a year. I'm certain my brother offered more than enough to make up for a year of your life, and he'll take care of the baby as well."

Elliot's right. I know that. But I need Ryder's trust if I'm going to do it. It's the least I want from him, and I don't even know how to articulate that so I don't end up sounding like a whiner.

"If you have...feelings for him, you should tell him," Elliot says, his eyes gentle and understanding. "He doesn't do well with games."

"Like that woman." The bitter words tumble out of me before I can stop myself.

"Yeah. Like Lauren. But that was a long time ago. Even if she left scars, that doesn't mean he's unsalvageable."

We talk for a while longer, but don't make much progress. Elliot finally gets up. "I'll show myself out. Just think about what I said...but if you really aren't going to go through with the wedding, tell him now. He's going to need to come up with a contingency bride."

Ryder

IF I HAD THINGS MY WAY, I WOULD'VE BEEN UP and out early this morning. Started drinking early, too, because alcohol is great for making me feel less bad about the crap in my life.

But Elliot isn't answering my calls. If I didn't know better, I'd assume he's avoiding me. *But why?*

He never does that. It's got to be Elizabeth getting in the middle of things. She can be pretty meddlesome when she puts her mind to it.

I'm already feeling like shit. *Guilty* shit. I shouldn't have told Paige that walking away meant it was over. She might've spent the night with Renni or Bethany and come back after cooling off a little. But I made it clear she couldn't come back…not unless she wanted to grovel.

Sighing, I rub my forehead. *Fucking Anthony*. The history between us—and knowing that he's plotting something—brings out the worst in me. It's like I can hardly think or speak rationally. For some reason, Paige refuses to believe Anthony is dangerous. But he's made it clear to me that he's going to pay me back for Lauren. It doesn't matter that she played both of us, did drugs…or that the Mexican authorities ruled her death an accident. He holds me responsible.

And I can't fault him for that. I just wish he'd come after *me*, not the people around me.

Elizabeth's already at the table by the time I go downstairs for a late lunch. She's in a bright red sundress that makes her look like a cardinal. The chef has made a salad, some garlic bread and cheese lasagna, and the housekeeper placed it all on a raised platform like an offering to the gods. My staff isn't stupid. They know what's happening, which is why we're having my favorite for lunch.

The second I take my seat, Elizabeth says, "You made a big mistake."

"You say that about everything I do."

"This time is especially bad. You know Paige didn't release that sex tape."

"It's not about the damn tape." I lean back in my seat. The lasagna suddenly looks about as appetizing as a brick on my plate.

She puts her fork down. "Then what is it?"

"She's in a snit over those flowers. The ones from Anthony."

She narrows her eyes, pursing her mouth. It's her *I know you* look. "You threw them out, didn't you?"

"The vase broke. What was I supposed to do?"

"*Reeeeaaaaally?*" She drags the vowel out. "How did *that* happen?"

I get up and get myself some scotch. If I can't eat, I'm going to drink. "The housekeeper knocked it off the table," I mutter.

"Ryder, what are you doing? Channeling Grandma Shirley?"

The name raises my hackles. You aren't supposed to speak ill of the dead, but she's an exception. The woman was positively evil. "I'm nothing like her."

"Let's see." Elizabeth raises a hand and starts counting on her fingers. "Proud. Autocratic. Determined to get your way no matter what.

Don't care that much about what others think or feel. Opinionated." She switches to her other hand. "Highly unlikely to change your mind about anything. Think you know better than the people around you… Shall I go on?"

My face warms at the list. She's not entirely wrong. I can be pretty autocratic, and I rarely take no for an answer. But anybody who's successful wouldn't, for god's sake.

"Instead of turning your relationship with Paige into a media circus, just call the wedding off. That's the best you can do for everyone."

"You don't know jack shit," I say.

"I know there's less than three weeks left before the ceremony." She sips her white wine. "And I know Paige is under a lot of pressure that has nothing to do with that tape."

"What pressure?" Maybe Paige told her something earlier.

"Don't you check social media?"

"Of course not. Why would I?" I have accounts, of course, but they're managed by pros. I only share a few photos if I ever feel like it, and I prefer to stay away from people as much as possible. Give them a taste, and they want to devour you. I'm not doing that, and I don't need to hustle to cultivate a fan base or be authentic or whatever the hell the so-called gurus recommend. I'm already a star.

"You should. It's ugly for Paige, and unlike you, I bet she doesn't have people taking care of that for her."

I curse under my breath. None of this would've been an issue if Paige had let my team handle her publicity, including taking over her social media. The thing is, I'm pretty certain she didn't release the tape either. But it's impossible to talk to her rationally when she gives me ultimatums or sits there cooing over Anthony's flowers. And she knows how those actions will push my buttons. She's been with me too long not to.

I have another scotch.

"You should eat," Elizabeth says, eyeing my untouched food. "I know you skipped dinner last night."

"Keeping track of me, Mother?"

Two beats of silence. "Ass."

The single word, muttered under her breath, stops me. "Excuse me?"

"What?" Her voice is tart.

"You said 'ass.'"

"So?"

"You cursing is like, is like…" I can't even think of a good comparison. "Like Mother Theresa making porn," I say at last.

"Well, what's a girl to do when her brother's being a bone-head?"

"Fine. I'll eat."

I manage to shovel a few forkfuls down my throat and begin to feel slightly better. Eventually I finish every bite. I have to admit, it makes a difference.

But as soon as I finish I get up and leave, not bothering to wait for dessert. I don't want to sit there and bear the waves of disapproval pouring out of Elizabeth.

Once I'm in my office, I lie down on the barcalounger and call my agent. She bitched about the surprise engagement, so she can hear about how things are going. Besides, she's a good problem solver, and unlike Elizabeth, she doesn't talk about how I'm like Shirley…possibly because she never met Grandma.

"You didn't tell me Paige was pregnant," Mira says.

"We wanted to announce it after the wedding."

"Hmmm… Well, too late now." She waits a beat. "Is the baby okay?"

"Yeah, it's fine." Or so Paige said.

"I heard you had an altercation at the hospital."

I make a face, remembering the crazy nurse. "Yeah. Some psycho fan. At least she didn't come after me with a Jeep."

"Hospitals have lots of sharp objects. I should have our attorney contact them. It's unacceptable."

"Handle it without making a big deal about it."

"Will do."

"And Mira?"

"Yes?"

"Paige moved out. Thought you should know now rather than find out because some idiot posted something about it somewhere."

"*What?*"

"We're taking a break. That's how we should spin it. Or maybe she wants to spend some time with her friends or something."

"Why did she move out?"

"It's complicated." I'm not telling Mira about the whole ugly mess. It's private, and none of her business.

"She can't do this. I don't care how complicated it is."

"You won't interfere," I growl. "I'm going to handle it."

"How?" Mira growls louder, like we're in some ursine competition. "If I'd known she was going to be this unreliable, I would've never suggested that you marry her, even for a year. God. How could I have misjudged her?"

For some reason, her irate tone and words annoy me. "You didn't misjudge Paige. The spotlight was probably too much for her."

"Ha! Do fish complain about too much water?"

My jaw flexes. Mira isn't saying anything I haven't thought, but it still pisses me off to hear the words out loud. I didn't call her to listen to her go off on Paige. I need to get her back because the wedding is going to happen no matter what. She told me to find somebody more to my liking, but she doesn't understand why I have to marry ASAP.

Technically, Dad gave all of us six months to find somebody and get hitched. I'm not worried about most of my siblings, but Lucas may be a problem. He made it clear he wasn't interested, and unless all of us fulfill the conditions, none of us will get the portraits.

He needs to see that it's no big deal to marry. It's only for a year anyway. And I need to set the example since I'm the one least likely to settle down. Everyone knows my reputation and all the women I've "humped and dumped."

"If she isn't going to marry you, you should cut her off completely. No monthly allowance and no medical. That would serve her right," Mira says. "And speaking of cutting, we need to do something about that idiot temp assistant you have. Every time I talk to him, I feel like I'm losing IQ points."

I jerk upright in my seat. "You're a genius."

"I know, but I can handle only so much incompetence and stupidity. At the rate it's going, I'm gonna—"

"I gotta go."

"What? Wait."

"And you can fire the temp." I hang up.

Unable to sit still, I jump up and start pacing. Of course! Why didn't I think of it before? Paige needs income and medical insurance to get through her pregnancy.

It's probably the best leverage I have. And while Elizabeth might be right about my being an ass, I'm not letting it go to waste.

NINE

Paige

Bethany's car isn't starting this morning, so we take my Altima to her office. After arriving, I spend an hour in an empty cubicle, reading and trying to relax. Then I walk the few blocks to the offices of Jones & Jones. Once this meeting is over, I'll go back and get Bethany so we can go home together after lunch. She's only working four hours today.

Marble, sunlight and the smell of stratospheric levels of success pervade the lobby of Jones & Jones. Ryder's attorney, Samantha Jones sent me a text requesting a meeting. I hit the elevator button and take a deep breath. She probably wants to talk about the prenup.

The wedding is definitely off, and I assume that means Ryder's and my prenup becomes invalid. But maybe there are still papers that I have to sign to cancel it or something.

Ryder's parting words about what walking out would mean still ring in my ears. Given how he isn't going to compromise or change, I know in my mind that I did the right thing.

Now if I could just convince my heart, I'd be all set.

A well-groomed receptionist stands up when she spots me. She gives me a standard I'm-doing-my-job smile. "Hello Ms. Johnson. Everyone's waiting."

She leads me down the hall to the conference room where Ryder and I first came for our prenup discussion with Samantha. Despite her disapproval, he insisted I take his money to ensure my child's future. And my own as well.

It feels odd to realize that this is how it's going to end between us. We should've never tried to fake a wedding and all the other stuff. It's partly my fault for wanting to marry rather than just admit to Mom and Simon that I was pregnant. Shame and the need for approval can make people do really stupid things.

I walk into the room. The monolithic conference table still dominates, chairs surrounding it like sunflower petals. The air has the same faint smell of fresh wax and paper.

My gaze falls on the chair where I sat last time. God, the memory heats my face. Ryder pushed me onto the table and gave me not only the hottest orgasm I've ever had, but the hottest one I could ever imagine. I climaxed so hard and fast, I finally understood why the French call it *the little death*.

Ryder is sitting at the table now, and something dark and knowing passes in his eyes. He doesn't say anything, though…just picks up a pitcher and pours water into an empty glass.

He's wearing a power suit—the dark navy with chocolate pinstripes. The color darkens his eyes to an Atlantic ultramarine. His steel-gray silk tie is knotted perfectly, and an air of dynastic opulence and wealth surrounds him. It says he expects the world to turn as he wills.

Of course I know he doesn't really expect such things. I've seen his struggles, know his issues. You don't work with somebody for close to half a decade and not notice. But his charisma is such that I almost forget all that as I look at him.

Unlike him, I'm in a cream-colored tunic and a dark brown skirt with silver flowers that ends an inch over my knees. The only accessories I have on are my pearl earrings and the one-of-a-kind engagement ring he gave me.

I sit across from him. "Where's Samantha?"

"Not coming." He pushes the glass of water my way.

I frown. "Are we rescheduling?"

"Nope. We don't need her to talk about what we need to talk about."

"You could've called."

He raises an eyebrow. "So you can ignore me?"

I look away. "You said it was over." I don't care what Elliot said. He can't possibly know everything between me and Ryder. Besides, Elliot's always going to be on his brother's side.

"You walked out."

"You forced me into the position."

"And all over some flowers." He mutters something that sounds suspiciously like "for fuck's sake."

"To you they were flowers. To me, they symbolized the dictatorial way you're approaching our relationship." I shake my head slightly. "Approached."

The muscles in his jaw tense for a moment, then he shrugs. "Anyway, I'm not here to fight."

"Then what do you want?" He could've summoned me here for all sorts of reasons. My best guess is to find a way to end the wedding and who's going to be responsible for the deposits and expenses so far. He said he'd take care of the ceremony, but that was when we were actually going to do it. I don't know how he feels about paying for everything now, and frankly, I'd prefer to pay part of it myself so I don't have anything hanging over me. I hate owing people.

"If you aren't going to marry me, you should at least continue as my assistant," he says.

Shock ripples through me. "Are you serious?"

"I'm always serious about work."

I shake my head. "I can't just…*continue*, as if the last few weeks never happened."

"You have a different job lined up?"

"No. I'm looking, though."

"Might be hard to find one," he observes. "You're kind of notorious at the moment."

My hands tighten into fists. I hate it when people point out what I'm trying very hard to deny. "Is that damned tape going to haunt me for the rest of my life?"

"Nah," he says with a shrug. "People will forget about it when juicier news comes around. Ten years from now, and it'll be like it never existed."

Damn you, Shaun.

"But even without the sex tape, you won't find a new job anytime soon." He gestures at my belly. "You're pregnant."

I rub my forehead. It's starting to hurt now.

Ryder continues, "You're going to need income and medical insurance. Prenatal care isn't cheap, and Dr. Silverman doesn't even accept insurance. Her practice is strictly on a concierge basis."

This is bad news. Really bad. Dr. Silverman is the best doctor I've ever had. She actually spends time with me and listens to my concerns and discusses everything in detail. And with the bleeding I had earlier, I would vastly prefer to have her providing me with the care my baby and I need.

"But if you come back to your old job, I can pay for all that," Ryder continues. "She'll be better for you and the baby anyway."

The offer is tempting, but I'm not convinced he has no ulterior motive. He can be unexpectedly sweet, but I've also seen him at his devious best—or worst—when he's fixated on getting his way. "Why are you doing this?"

He looks toward the ceiling and a slow smile spreads over his face. "I'm tired of dealing with my own mail?" He looks at me, squinting slightly, to see if I'm going to go for the ploy.

The gall of the man. "Try again."

The smile vanishes, and silence stretches. Then he finally sighs. "Okay." He leans forward, placing his linked hands on the table. "Look, Paige. We've wasted enough time being at odds with each other. Frankly, I don't like that. We've never fought like this before, and I don't understand why it's happening now. I mean, all we're trying to do is the right thing for each other. Right? A temporary marriage would solve both our problems, and it'd be so damn neat." He clears his throat. "And I'm sorry for saying that it would be over if you walked out. Once I calmed down, it was obvious you needed some time to cool off."

"So you think the problem is our tempers?" My teeth grind together. "That I'm just…pissy?"

"What else can it be?"

"Your idea of a relationship between us is, you issue an order and I obey regardless of how I feel about it. I didn't realize it until we hit that bump." I pause, taking a moment to collect myself. "You said we needed to put on a good show. But I'm not an actor like you, Ryder. I can't fake things I don't feel. I just…can't."

"So it's a no?" His voice lacks all inflection.

"I…" I stop.

If it were just me, I'd say no. I don't want to risk hurting myself anymore. It cut deep when he thought the worst of me based on his experience with Lauren, and it kept bleeding when he continued to act like I was betraying him by being civil to Anthony, who's probably just as plugged in as everyone else and saw the news and decided to send flowers as an apology. There was no reason for me to reject that. I'd prefer that Ryder and Anthony reconcile rather than keep on with the hostility because of what happened with a woman who's been dead and buried for a while now.

But I have a baby to consider. I can't stay at Bethany's place indefinitely. After all, she's expecting too. And I can't go home to Sweet Hope, not for a while. That town is full of busybodies who'll sniff around shamelessly for every morsel of gossip.

And as much as I hate to admit it, I need the best care money can buy. That means Ryder is my best chance. But god…I *hate* it that I'm being forced into making a decision I'm not sure about due to circumstances beyond my control.

"If you don't want to make up your mind right now, tell me tomorrow," he says. "Or you can just simply move back in."

"Move back in?"

"All your stuff is at my place, and you're better off there anyway. Better security and privacy. If you want, you can take the guest house."

Like that's going to make any real difference. I exhale with frustration. "Do you really want to do this?"

"I do."

Without thinking, I rest a hand on my belly. "All right. I'll call you tomorrow."

Ryder

I LET OUT A HEAVY SIGH WHEN THE DOOR CLOSES behind Paige. If Mira knew how unprepared I was, she would've yelled at me. *When you go into a negotiation, you have to know exactly what you want to get out of it…and when you're going to walk away from the deal.* How many times has she told me that?

The only thing I knew was that I wanted Paige back somehow and that I wasn't going to walk away. No matter what.

Does this mean I can actually pretend that the sex tape and all that shit never happened? No. But I'm willing to deal with the fallout. I have an entire team for that. What I can't handle is how cavernous and empty my house felt after Paige left.

I get up and leave. When I get to the lobby, not only do the receptionist's eyes soften, her entire face melts into the usual "you're so dreamy" look. More or less on auto-pilot, I shoot her an empty grin I've perfected over the years…but I keep on walking. If we'd met before Paige and I decided to get married, I might've considered banging her. But now not even a whiff of interest stirs inside me.

The elevator bank is empty. Guess Paige already went down to the lobby. I'm confident she'll say yes. After all, a baby is kind of the ultimate leverage. I should probably feel bad about that, but I don't. I'm willing to fight that dirty.

I'm parked in the garage on the next block. I step out of the building and immediately stop. There's some kind of commotion going on, and the security guards have left their station to gawk.

"What's going on?" I ask an older guy in a suit who's walking past.

He glances back. "Fight. Some girl and a bunch of other people."

I shake my head and think about going a different way to my car. I like rubbernecking as much as the next person, but I can't afford to get involved in a street fight. Then I see a familiar figure in the throng.

Tall, with dark hair and a slim but lean frame, Anthony is in the middle. There's something white smeared on his face, and my jaw loosens. I've never seen him in a brawl, ever.

Unable to stop myself, I start walking toward the scene. The crowd vibrates with righteous anger or something close to it.

"Slut!"

"You fat bitch! You aren't that special!"

The epithets continue. Most of them are pretty pedestrian, but the tone makes them unusually vicious. I recognize a bouncer from the club with Anthony. Based on the cuss words, the people aren't trying to attack *him*. So why is he in the middle of it?

Then I see. The golden hair pulled back in a ponytail and the back of a cream shirt and brown skirt.

My brain takes no time at all. It's obvious what's going on. The sleeve of Paige's tunic is torn, and there's some kind of red sauce on her face.

I run down and put myself between Paige and the screeching sociopaths. The crowd isn't all women. A fair number of them are men, and they throw out words to egg on the women. Some of them have their phones out to record the incident.

Not a single one tries to help Paige. Well. Except for Anthony and his bouncer.

I feel something cold land on the back of my neck. I drag Paige back to the lobby. "Close the fucking doors and do your job!" I shout at the idiotic security guards.

As if my order snaps them out of a dream, they jump and block the people from following us in. Anthony and the bouncer guy are allowed inside, probably because the guards saw them helping Paige before.

Her eyes are a little glassy, and she's shaking. I wrap my arms around her, not caring about the sauce and other crap. Her heart beats against mine like a frightened bird's, and helplessness and fury twist into an ugly knot.

"What the hell happened?" I snarl at nobody in particular. It's that or go out and start beating the shit out of people. I'm not the kind of guy who likes to beat people up for just kicks—that honor goes to one of my cousins—but this is different.

"Someone cast the first stone," Anthony murmurs.

"What?"

"At first, those people were only taking photos and verbally harassing her. They got more aggressive when she shielded her face and tried to ignore them. Finally, one of them threw something at her—"

"A leftover hotdog," the bouncer says.

"—and it escalated from there. As I said, the first stone."

Of course. "Fuck. I'm pressing charges."

Anthony grimaces and runs his hands down his shirt and slacks. They're ruined, but somehow he still manages to look elegant. "A nasty bodyguard would be faster and easier," he says, glancing toward his enormous associate.

"Nobody asked you," I say, even though I know it isn't his fault. He helped Paige, and the good manners drilled into me all my life say I should thank him, but my internal alarm won't shut up. *Anthony helping Paige out of the goodness of his heart?* Nope. I don't buy it.

He shrugs, but ignores me otherwise. The bouncer wears a bland expression, like this is par for the course.

I pull out a handkerchief and wipe Paige's face. "You can't go back to your sister's. It may not be safe." I stop and swallow. "Why didn't you tell me it was this bad?"

"It wasn't. Not…before."

"Shit."

Tremors run through me, and shame unfurls in the deepest part of my gut. Paige mentioned something about haters, but I never thought it was that big a deal. I took her safety for granted, the way I do my own. I have my share of crazy stalkers and psychos, but except for one crazy woman who tried to run me over, most would never dare attack me like this. Not in public, or in broad daylight. They just don't have the courage to confront a tall, broad-shouldered man in his prime.

"Come on. Come home." I have to have her under my roof where she'll be safe. "You can move into the guest house. I don't care. I can't let you be out here by yourself. You were going to accept my proposal anyway."

As soon as the words leave my mouth, I know I screwed up. Her eyes focus with hard-edged annoyance, and she stiffens. "Even now? That's what you're thinking about?"

Of course not, but I don't have the time or patience to convince her. I wish she were a little bit more like the vapid women who usually cling to me. "Paige... I phrased it wrong, but you know what I mean. You can't be out here on your own."

"Fortunately, she doesn't have to," Anthony says. "She can stay at my penthouse. I can assign TJ here to her for protection."

I bare my teeth. "Over my dead body."

"Oh, calm down. Unlike you, I don't steal women. And I'm not going to be in town anyway. I'm leaving for Paris tonight."

Does that mean he's finished in L.A.? I'd love to have him be gone forever. That would leave me and Paige with one less issue.

Paige licks her lips, her gaze darting back and forth between me and Anthony.

Come on.

She nods at Anthony. "All right."

TEN

Paige

Anthony's penthouse isn't that far from downtown. He doesn't seem to mind that I soiled his car seat. I don't want to know how much it's going to cost to clean the leather.

He also didn't gloat in the face of Ryder's incredulous fury. I thought Ryder was going to take my wrist and drag me back to his Beverly Hills mansion anyway, but he somehow managed to restrain himself.

Given my interactions with Anthony, I assumed his place would be dark and gloomy. Instead it's airy and bright with a tall ceiling and lots of big windows. The walls are mostly barren. There are a few paintings that somehow don't count. I have the feeling that he bought them as investments rather than because he likes art.

They're framed and displayed in a professional but clinical manner. There aren't any books or movies or music either. The floor is pristine oak, shiny and blemish-free.

I shiver, but my chill has nothing to do with the air conditioning blowing in my direction. It's the sterility of the place. The glass-top tables and iron chairs only add to the lifeless appearance.

Unease runs a finger down my back.

"Don't worry," he says. "I don't collect moths, and there's no basement with a pit."

That startles me so much I snort a laugh.

"Are you all right?"

"As well as I can be. Thank you. And TJ, too."

"Ryder should've known better than to let you walk around unprotected."

I make a face. "Even if he'd offered, I would've turned him down. I'm not into chaperones."

Anthony grunts. "You should shower. There's a bathroom you can use in the guest suite, which is to your right. Unfortunately, I don't have much in the way of clothes you can borrow. But I'll call housekeeping to do your laundry."

"I can do it myself. Thanks."

I go into the guest suite. A four-poster king-size bed sits in the center. Two bedside lamps are mounted on the wall above small tables with drawers. Other than that, the room doesn't have anything. The en suite bathroom alone is easily bigger than Bethany and Oliver's master bedroom. The separate shower and tub dominate the space. The double vanity looks so pristine, it's like nobody's ever used it. The frosted glass stall has some kind of European shampoo and conditioner, plus a body soap. I wash quickly. The combination of ketchup, mustard and grease has filmed over my skin, and I scrub extra hard to get rid of it completely.

I come out of the bathroom wrapped in an oversized towel and see a black t-shirt with the Z logo on the bed. It's obviously one of Anthony's. I run my teeth over my lower lip and shift my weight. If it had been Ryder's, I wouldn't think twice about putting it on, but… It feels wrong, like a bride wearing a ring from a man who isn't her groom.

However, the other option is putting on the dirty clothes, which is no option at all. Now I regret coming to Anthony's place. I only decided to do it because going to Ryder's home when he obviously expected me to—practically demanded me to—seemed like giving in. Plus, I was furious with him. I've made it clear that I can't be with him if he doesn't trust me…or treats me like the hired help rather than someone he's actually in a relationship with. The fact that our "marriage" is only going to last a year doesn't change how I feel, especially if he wants me to act the part of a devoted and besotted wife.

I sit next to the shirt. If Ryder had just said he'd decided to trust me, I might've gone with him. He's an easy guy to crush on, and as much as I don't want to admit it, I have feelings for him. It's just that my pride and self-respect won't let me let those feelings control me to the point that I'll let him walk all over me.

Marriage and money or no, I don't want to change who I am deep inside to suit his every whim. My earliest memories are about Mom being in relationship after relationship with men who were suitable only as providers of a roof and food. Those men never appreciated the fact that she always gave into their demands and put their needs first. In fact, the more she accommodated them the less they respected her.

But after watching Simon and Mom together, I know a healthy relationship is about give and take. I won't give and give and give the way Mom did with those toxic jerks.

I blow out a breath, annoyed with myself. "Stop thinking and stop hiding." I throw on the shirt and look for a hair dryer, but all the drawers in the bathroom are empty. I towel it dry as well as I can and put on my pumps. They look ridiculous with the T-shirt, even though it's long enough to practically be a dress, but I want to cover as much skin as possible. My shield if you will. Then I finally go out into the living room.

Anthony's already showered, and his hair is still damp too. He's sitting at the counter in a white button-down shirt and dark slacks much like the ones he was wearing before. His gaze sweeps over me, and a grin pops on his face as he takes note of my shoes. "The shirt looks good on you. Keep it if you like."

I flush with discomfort. "I'll launder it and send it back."

"Whatever you like." He twists the cap off a bottle of mineral water. "Something to drink?"

"No, thank you," I say, staying in the same spot. I rest a hip against the couch arm. It too is pristine white.

He doesn't make any move to come closer. "How's the baby?"

The sudden change in topic throws me off. "What?"

"Your unborn child. Is it well? I never heard anything about what happened at the ER, and obviously they aren't going to tell me anything."

"Um…yeah. It's fine."

He nods. Something like regret crosses his face, but his features settle back into a blank façade again. "If I'd known you were pregnant…" His lips turn bloodless as he presses them together and he shakes his head slightly.

"You were fighting." I shrug. "You wouldn't have been able to help yourself."

"You sound so kind, but still manage to make me look like a monster."

"You and Ryder are being monstrous to each other over a woman who died years ago. I'm not sure how I'm supposed to make any of it sound enlightened."

"Touché." He sips his water. "Do you plan to leave him?"

"You'd like that, wouldn't you?"

"Like?" He considers. "No. But it would amuse me." He puts the water bottle down. "Whatever Ryder has dangled in front of you to get you back, I can match it."

He has no idea what Ryder's offered. I highly doubt Anthony would claim my baby as his just to keep it out of Shaun's reach. Besides, who would believe it was his anyway? "Seems like the people who don't like Ryder tend to be pretty predictable."

Anthony arches an eyebrow. "Did you get another offer?"

"Yes."

A mild amusement lights his eyes for a moment. "Let me guess. Julian."

I say nothing. He can guess all he wants.

"Ryder's father has always been an asshole," Anthony says.

That I can agree with, not that I'd let him know.

"You see…you have a weak point that makes Ryder's enemies think they can use you."

"I don't have a weak point."

"Oh, please." His gaze drops to my stomach. "Your baby. It is the weakest of points for mothers, highly exploitable." A sardonic smile twists his mouth. "Well. Most mothers anyway. And I have a feeling you're one of the typical ones."

"You won't be able to use it to get back at Ryder," I say.

"If I wanted to get back at him, to even the scales, as it were…I'd've made sure you lost it."

I suck in a sharp breath. My hand flies to cover my belly protectively.

The muscles in his jaw grow taut as he looks at my hand. "Oh yes. I lost a baby because of him."

The harsh announcement hits me hard. "What…?"

"Lauren was pregnant when she finally told me about Ryder. At that time, I begged her to keep the child, but she wouldn't hear of it. Said she couldn't afford to fritter away a career opportunity with something as inconvenient as a baby. Now that I think about it, I don't even know if it was really mine, but back then I thought it was." The skin around his eyes tightens, and his entire face looks like a mask.

Suddenly, the evening takes on an ominous tone. I start shaking. "Are you going to hurt me to get back at Ryder?"

"Perhaps I should." He turns the bottle in his hand, studying it.

My blood turns to ice, and I clench the hand over my belly until it's a tight fist.

"Except…I didn't feel even a kernel of satisfaction when I heard about your hospital visit." He looks up and locks eyes with me.

A moment passes before I lick my dry lips and rasp out, "That makes you a good person. It isn't something to be conflicted about."

"But I don't want to be good, Paige." He closes his eyes for a moment, then gets off the stool, walking over to a window and a view of the city outside. "I want my pound of flesh."

I don't have an answer for that. Telling him it'd do his soul good to give up his revenge just seems corny, a cliché from a badly written redemption flick.

"I want to know how much pressure I can exert before your relationship implodes and you decide he isn't worth it. After all, that's how Ryder got Lauren to leave me…by convincing her

I wasn't worth it." He doesn't turn to look at me. "Make yourself comfortable. I need to get going."

"Thank you," I say automatically, even as my mind is reeling.

"Oh, don't thank me. I'm not doing this to be nice."

The door closes behind him.

TJ ARRIVES SOON AFTER ANTHONY LEAVES. THE bouncer is huge, with big muscles like pale slabs of butcher beef and an even bigger attitude. He doesn't hide the fact that he's a bad ass and he knows it.

Of course I've known him for a few years at Z, so none of that impresses me.

His gaze doesn't drop below my neck. "You okay? Need me to call a doc or something?"

"I'm fine."

He grunts and lowers himself onto the other couch. "Lemme know if you need anything."

My phone rings. It's Bethany.

"My gosh, are you all right?" she says the second I hit the green button.

"Yes," I say even as I wonder how many more calls I'm going to get. There's Mom and Simon… Renni too.

"I was wondering what was taking so long, then my coworker told me he saw you on YouTube! I can't believe it! Did you call the police? You should press charges. They need to pay. It's unacceptable. They weren't just hurting you but your baby too. It's like double assault!"

I let her rant. She'll have to get it out of her system before she can carry on a rational conversation. I catch TJ in my peripheral vision and walk out onto the balcony, closing the door behind me. He doesn't need to hear our conversation.

While she fires off a hundred words a minute, I take in the view. The city goes on like nothing major's happened. The people who attacked me are probably down there somewhere. Are they proud of themselves? Are they going to pretend they didn't do anything wrong?

Finally Bethany slows down. "Okay. Okay. So." She sounds breathless.

"So."

"Are you at Ryder's?"

"No."

"Paige! You can't just go to your apartment! You have to find a secure, safe place. Preferably with gates and guards."

"Um, actually—"

"I said you could stay with us as long as you want, but I don't know if I can keep you safe. I'd feel better if you went back to Ryder." Anxiety adds force and speed to her words. "I saw how his mansion was. I'm sure nobody can get to you there."

"Actually, I'm at Anthony's."

That puts the brakes on her. "Who?"

"Someone I know," I say, being a bit vague. "He owns Z," I add, hoping that associating him with something she knows is legitimate will alleviate her worry.

"I see." A short pause. "So...why are you with him and not Ryder?" Her voice doesn't contain any censure, but it isn't exactly approving either. I would say she's concerned and maybe even a little worried.

I sigh. "It's complicated." And probably poorly thought out. Now that I know the depth of Lauren's betrayal, I'm not at all certain it's a smart idea for me to stay with Anthony.

"Paige, are you one hundred percent sure about breaking things off with Ryder?"

I can't answer her. I thought that would be best, but when he came for me in the midst of chaos... I've never seen him so worried or concerned. As trite as it sounds, he looked like an avenging angel coming to save me, eyes flashing and fists pumping. He threw himself into the crowd without any worry for his own safety or his image or...anything.

"Ryder offered me a job," I blurt out. I'd been thinking about it when those people decided to mob me. Otherwise I might've been more aware of my surroundings.

"He did?"

"Yeah. He said I'm going to need the money and benefits, which is true. He even offered to pay for my obstetrician. She's amazing, but she doesn't take insurance."

Bethany's quiet for a moment. "Do you want to go back to working for him?"

"No. Well, yes." I sigh. "I don't know." I rest my elbows on the railing and cup my forehead in my free hand. "He didn't say anything I hadn't already thought of. It's going to be so much harder for me to get a job with the…scandal and being pregnant and all. And even though I think I've been awesome at my job, he can always find somebody else. I'm not arrogant enough to think I'm irreplaceable. And I do need some money, and I *have* to have insurance."

"Is that all there is?"

"What do you mean?"

"You didn't tell me everything, and I'm sure there's stuff I can't understand since I'm not the one in the relationship with him. And I've never dated anybody that famous or high-profile. But before you make any final decisions, don't just think about the bad things, but the good things as well. I had my doubts when I heard you were engaged to Ryder, but when I saw how he looked at you and defended you against his stepmother at the dinner…" She trails off. I can imagine her eyebrows pinching. She always does that when she's debating or thinking. "It made me feel good about you and Ryder. Mom and Dad thought so, too."

"They did?" Simon thought Ryder was a womanizing jerk. Okay, maybe not quite a jerk, but something pretty close.

"Yeah. I spoke with them at the party. Dad said he felt a bit relieved about the two of you."

That's news to me. I had no idea.

"Paige, all relationships require work. It's just that…sometimes the payoff isn't worth it. So if you feel that way about Ryder, then I support your decision to end the relationship. If not, then…"

"But he doesn't trust me, Bethany," I say. "That's why I thought it'd be better if we stop now, before we go too far."

She thinks about that for a few moments. "Did he *say* he doesn't trust you?"

"The tape." I swallow. Just thinking about it leaves me shaking with rage and humiliation. "He thought I released it."

Bethany gasps. "Is he insane?"

"No. It's just his experience. That's what women in Hollywood do."

"But you're not, you know… One of them."

"Not to Ryder. To him, every woman wants to be famous." I rest my chin in my palm. "I feel like he and I just…went over the same territory again and again. Ever since the tape was released, we kept talking about it without ever coming to a decision."

"But you didn't really have a chance. You were at the hospital, and now this."

Suddenly tired, I close my eyes. Bethany is probably right. Ryder and I have gone through so many experiences since the night of our engagement party, charged with high emotions, most of them dark and ugly.

Bethany huffs out a breath audibly. "That job he offered… Is it your old job?"

"Yes."

"So if he doesn't trust you, why would he do that? It doesn't make sense. You're going to be able to access all his information."

I pause. That never occurred to me, but Bethany's right. He doesn't hire anybody without vetting them thoroughly first and making them sign a non-disclosure agreement.

So maybe… Maybe Ryder *does* trust me after all, but he just doesn't quite know it yet or hasn't transitioned from "I trust Paige my Assistant" to "I trust Paige my Bride-to-Be."

I gaze out at the LA cityscape. In spite of calling me babe and having me clean up his messes, he's always treated me with respect. He never questioned the way I did my job or let anybody else boss me around. Not even Mira could treat me like the hired help in front of Ryder. And after we decided to marry for a year, he kept his promise to ensure I was never humiliated or hurt. I look down at the gorgeous engagement ring. He didn't have to go that far, but he did. He made sure I'll have sufficient funds after our divorce to be comfortable. He never once raised his voice or acted out in anger until Shaun released the sex tape.

He's reacting to Lauren's betrayal. It's really not you.

Maybe he's trying to make amends in the only way he knows how. For all his popularity and good looks, he can be clueless at times, and he is very careful about giving too much of himself to anybody. It isn't surprising, given what I know. His folks easily win the Worst Parents of All Time award, and his grandmother sounds like a horror show. If she was even remotely like Ryder's mother, I'm certain the older woman never hid the fact that she thought Ryder was retarded.

"Paige? You're awfully quiet," Bethany says.

"Yeah… You've given me a lot to think about."

"All helpful, I hope?"

"Of course." I smile my first true smile since Shaun released the tape. "Thank you."

I can't fix the pain we've suffered, but I can certainly do something about our future. I go back inside.

TJ looks up from his phone, raising an eyebrow.

I inhale deeply. "I'm going home."

ELEVEN

Ryder

"Is Paige all right?" Elliot asks, a glass of scotch in his hand. He came over when he heard—or to be more precise *saw*—what happened outside Jones & Jones. The assholes who filmed the fight uploaded the clip everywhere, and it's not even five. I don't get the motivation behind doing such things, but maybe posting it on YouTube is supposed to be more heroic than helping the victim.

Sinking deeper into the living room couch that faces the garden, I drink my scotch. It burns. Too bad it can't burn away the nasty taste in the back of my throat. "As far as I know."

"And you?"

"I'm not the one who got attacked."

"You shielded her…"

"Not the same thing." My voice is terse.

Elliot shakes his head. "How did it happen?"

"I have no idea. Paige left first. When I got to the lobby, she was already outside and the attack had started."

"Damn." He knocks back his scotch. "Mira was right after all."

"About what?"

"She said when a woman has sex, she's a slut. And when a woman is labeled a slut, she's fair game."

Elliot isn't saying anything I didn't know. I've seen how female celebrities end up being a Public Target Number One. But Paige isn't a celebrity. "I had no idea it was this bad for her."

"She never complained?"

"Once. A little bit." She told me the only reason she agreed to the interview with Derek Madison was to tell her side of the story because she was tired of people making stuff up about her, portraying her badly. I rejected that explanation, telling myself she just wanted to be famous.

I squeeze my eyes shut. How could I have been so wrong?

Elliot wisely says nothing for a moment, letting me stew in self-recrimination. "She's just being targeted more because she doesn't fit the image of a deserving woman."

Raising my head, I look at him. "What the hell does that mean?"

"You know. She's not model gorgeous, not from a rich or famous family, not a size zero, didn't go to some fancy school, and didn't have some kind of noble job."

"What the hell is a 'noble' job?"

"Like feeding children or advocating for abused women or whatever."

My face scrunches. Shallow, judgmental people piss me off. "First of all, Paige is gorgeous. It isn't my fault that people can't see that. And you don't have to be rich or famous or a size zero, or have an Ivy League diploma to be worthy. If that's the criteria, people should pelt *me* with eggs and tomatoes." I have the looks, wealth and a famous family behind me, but I don't have anything else.

"But you're a guy."

"So?"

"So it's okay. The requirement is only for women."

"What the fuck?"

He shrugs. "Just how it is. Society is harsh on women. You know that."

I let my head fall back onto the thick cushion. Chandeliers hang from the high ceilings in the living room, one of them right over my position. It infuriates me that she's being treated unfairly and that I had no idea all this time. I promised her I would ensure she wasn't humiliated or hurt by our arrangement, and I failed to keep my word.

My phone pings with a text. I ignore it. I don't want to talk to anybody right now. If it's urgent, they can call.

"That might be Paige," Elliot says.

"No, it isn't. It's probably some junk."

He raises an eyebrow. "Where is she?"

"Not here."

"Oh." He nods sagely. The thing I like about him is that he knows me well. But sometimes he knows me too well. "Is she at her actress friend's?"

"No." The word grates out. If it were so, there wouldn't be that nasty taste lingering in the back of my throat.

"Are you guys okay?"

I consider. I don't want to answer him since it isn't anything pretty, and I feel like if I say it out loud, it's going to become real—a reality I won't be able to ignore.

There's no way to spin her decision to accept Anthony's offer. She might as well have sliced my balls off. A dark apprehension in my gut say she's also going to turn down my proposal at Samantha's office. I shove it down deeper before it makes me do something rash.

"Ryder?"

A HOLLYWOOD BRIDE

I almost jump off the couch at the soft voice coming from behind me. I turn and blink. I didn't imagine it.

Paige.

She's in the same clothes she had on earlier, albeit freshly laundered. Still, the ketchup and mustard stains are visible on her top. The tear in the sleeve hasn't been mended.

Her face is bare, free of makeup, and her hair hangs limply over her shoulders. Something fragile lurks in her gaze, and my heart leaps to my throat.

I don't know what to say. People think that I never run out of perfect lines. I suppose that makes sense if they only know me through cinema. After all it's easy to be fearless on set. I have the words, emotions, and props. I know exactly how my costars are going to react.

But here, at this moment, I feel like a derelict actor who didn't bother to study his script. Sweat slickens my palms, and my brain works frantically to come up with something to say.

Elliot squeezes my shoulder, nods at Paige, and leaves.

Finally I manage, "I didn't know you were coming."

"It felt wrong to stay there." Paige's voice is barely a whisper. She meets my eyes for a brief moment then drops her gaze. "I shouldn't have gone with Anthony."

She doesn't have to say anything more.

I step forward and wrap my arms around her. The tightness in my chest eases, and I can breathe again. Unable to help myself, I bury my nose in her hair. I absorb her warmth and her softness and the sweet scent that is uniquely hers. Of all the women I know, she's the only one who can seem to comfort my soul. What my brain and experience tell me means nothing when I feel like this, a weary man finding sanctuary.

Does it matter that the sanctuary may be temporary?

"You made the right decision," I rasp out. "Welcome home."

THE DINNER OFFERINGS COULD BE DESCRIBED AS, well, masculine. The chef initially prepared it for me and Elliot.

The lamb chops are amazing, a fresh mint sauce really bringing out the flavor of the meat. I realize how little I've eaten all day, which isn't like me. And the potatoes, garnished with some sort of green flecks that kind of look like mint but aren't, are excellent as well.

In deference to Paige's condition, I forgo a glass of cabernet, opting for ginger ale instead. To be honest, I'd prefer some scotch to loosen up the small knot in my gut. Even though she's back, I can't really relax. She hasn't mentioned my proposal back at Samantha's office, and there's the whole unresolved "if you don't trust me, we shouldn't marry" business.

"Don't force yourself to eat this. We can always get you something else," I say, watching Paige cut the meat with care. I don't recall her liking lamb before. She's more a steak and chicken kind of girl. Besides, she's entirely too pale, with circles under her eyes so dark they almost look like bruises. I can't help but think I've contributed to that by being stubborn. I've probably been a terrible dickhead if Elizabeth felt compelled to call me the a-word.

"But why? This is fine." She pops a small piece into her mouth and chews.

"I don't want you to get sick afterwards." My eyebrows pinch together as I study her expression for any signs of distaste. "I know you're supposed to be all nauseous and everything when you're pregnant."

The smile she gives me is bemused. Warmth unfurls in my chest, and some of the ugliness that's built up since the night of our engagement party ebbs away.

"Not everyone suffers from morning sickness," she tells me. "I've been okay so far. And the doctor at the hospital didn't seem too worried about my diet."

That reminds me… "Have you seen Dr. Silverman?"

Paige shakes her head. "She's out of the country right now."

"When is she coming back?"

"Day after tomorrow. And I have an appointment with her at eleven."

"Okay. I'll take you in."

Her lips part, then she shakes her head. "You don't have to."

"I insist." I hesitate, then add, "I don't ever want to go through that again."

She gives me a small smile, but somehow it lacks the usual *umph*. "Agreed. Let's not."

I brush my thumb over the fleshy web between her thumb and forefinger. The touch isn't sexual. It's a silent combination of "thank you" and "I'll take care of you". Until Dr. Silverman clears Paige for active duty, I really shouldn't make a move, no matter how much my hormones urge me to remind her how good we can be together.

We've had too many things happen to stop us from really talking about the core issue of whether or not we can trust each other enough to go through with the wedding. It's not something we can just gloss over. Perhaps making a decision about it would help me sort out my feelings. I hate it when I'm in limbo like this.

"About the job," she begins.

I wave a hand. "I only used that to make you come back."

"Still. I'll do it, but I'm not sure about the wedding yet."

It feels remarkably like she just kicked me in the nuts. I take a moment to process things. "Why?"

She shrugs. "You explained it yourself. I'm going to need a job that provides benefits, and I'm not going to find another position with all this media circus around me and my pregnancy. Not in this town, anyway."

It's nice to have her seeing things my way. But what she's saying doesn't relieve me of the pain. Rather, it intensifies it, and I can't figure out why. She's just repeating what I told her. But I hate it anyway, and I feel like a man on the run, although from what I don't know.

Sighing, she lays down her utensils. "I'm not saying no, Ryder. But I want you to really think about why you can trust me if I'm your assistant, but you can't if I'm your fiancée."

The suggestion makes me blink. "What are you talking about?"

"You would never make somebody you don't trust your assistant. You were always very clear on that point."

"I don't understand what that has to do with you being my wife. You know I wouldn't have proposed if I didn't trust you."

"Yeah, I know. But still, the first thing that came to your mind when you heard about the sex tape wasn't *there must be an explanation for this*. You thought I did it to become famous."

"Are you ever going to forgive me for that?" I ask, my whole body numb.

"It isn't about forgiveness. It's about how it's going to be between us going forward. This matters to me, Ryder. So please. Take a moment and really think about what I'm saying."

"But we have less than three weeks before the wedding." I'm starting to feel a little panicked. What she's asking for isn't something I can come up with in the next twenty-four hours. But at the same time, I can't imagine marrying anybody but her. My mind just won't consider it.

"You're a smart man, Ryder. I'm sure you'll figure out the answer soon." She stands up.

I rise too. I haven't finished my lamb chops, but my appetite's gone. "Are you going back to your sister's?"

"No. I don't think that would be wise." She

hesitates. "If you don't mind, I was thinking about staying here."

The tightness in my gut loosens. "Of course you should stay here," I say. "Like I said…welcome home."

She gives me the same small careful smile I've been seeing all evening and goes to the third floor.

Rubbing my face, I grab some scotch. I so need to drink.

Jesus. Stop panicking. It won't solve anything.

I tap my fingers on the table as the scotch burns my throat. She's *here*—with *me*. And she's going to stay, at least for now. And she hasn't said no to our marriage.

When a woman is trying to make me jump through hoops just to see if she can do it, I can tell. That's not what's happening with Paige. She genuinely needs to know the answer to her question.

Thinking back on it, I have no clue why I didn't trust her on the night of our engagement party. I should have. Even if I wasn't sure, I should've at least given her the moral support she needed rather than demanding that she explain herself, like she was on trial or something.

It's a long time—and a large bottle—later when I finally go to bed. But I still don't have an answer.

TWELVE

Paige

THE NEXT MORNING, I CRACK MY EYES OPEN WITH a renewed sense of purpose. Since I told Ryder I'd go back to my job, I follow my standard routine. Get up. Shower. Get dressed and put on my conservative work makeup with a pink lip gloss.

The only difference is that I don't have a commute, and I eat breakfast at the counter in Ryder's kitchen.

Elizabeth is there already, munching on a piece of toast with extra jam. She's in another of her designer dresses, this time a magenta Armani. I saw it on display during my post-engagement shopping spree.

"Morning." She smiles at me over a mug of coffee. Her cup reads *Beauty Is What You Make of It*.

"Good morning." The chef places tea in front of me.

"Nice to have you back," she says with a smile.

"Thanks. Ryder around?"

"Probably still asleep. The housekeeper said he went to bed late." Then she adds, "He didn't go out with Elliot."

I laugh. Elizabeth is so sweet, and I can't help but love her more when she treats me like I'm a *real* fiancée for Ryder, even though she has to know the truth.

"By the way did you see the latest issue of *Lifestyle?*" she asks.

I shake my head. It's a fashion and high-society gossip magazine, and I don't read it.

"They did a feature on your wedding."

"What?" I blink. "We aren't even married yet."

"Oh, not like that. They have photos of some of the designs and motifs you're going to be using. They're gorgeous." She sighs. "The ceremony's going to look like a fairy princess dream come true."

A sense of unease tugs at me. People are already making a big deal about our ceremony, and I'm not even sure there's going to be one. The fallout… Good god. I can't imagine.

I finish my simple breakfast of a bagel and cream cheese and go to my office. It's still the same, despite my extended absence. The antique

Louis XIV desk, the armchairs, the view of the pool and the garden…and the über-expensive ergonomic desk chair that's set specifically to my body's dimensions. I pause at the sight of the barbed wired wall in the middle distance. I always thought it made Ryder's estate look like a prison compound. But after having been in the spotlight for a while, I have a new appreciation for it. Actually, it's a miracle Ryder hasn't razed the mansion and built a bunker.

After booting up my laptop, I find the article Elizabeth was talking about at breakfast. Sure enough, it's on the main page of *Lifestyle*'s website. The photos are stunning, displaying bridal whites and some lovely spring green shades. I scroll down to the end, then spot the first comment, from a user named *lifehack*.

What a waste when they're probably going to divorce within a year. It's not like the girl's hot enough to keep him. He'll get bored with her once the novelty of fatherhood wears off.

The rest of the comments, and there are hundreds, are much uglier. It's like *lifehack* set the tone for everyone else. The consensus seems to be that I am not worthy of any of this because I don't fit the image of "beautiful" and "glamorous". One of them even wrote, *Read that Ryder is behind some anonymous funding for animal shelters in NC. He really deserves better than this dog.*

Then one of them posts a meme with a manatee with my face photoshopped onto it. A wedding veil and flowers sit on my head. The caption reads *Paigatee*.

The picture is hideous, the photoshop work clumsy and obviously done on the fly, but the effect still knocks the breath out of me. My face heats, and the area around my eyes prickles.

But *Paigatee* isn't the end of it. There are more memes, each nastier than the one before, as though people are trying to one-up each other on the thread. Many of them also reference the sex tape, mocking my body because "who the hell would want to see a fat chick get laid?" Each comment comes with a "Report Abuse" button, but if I clicked all of them I'd give myself carpel tunnel.

Anger and resentment surge inside me like a tidal wave. My hands shake so hard, I have to curl them into fists. What have I done to deserve this kind of treatment?

A tight knot lodges in my throat, and I breathe audibly through my mouth. I need to calm down before I start hyperventilating and throw up.

The rational side of me understands that these people don't matter. They don't know me, and their opinions are ignorant and mean. They'll move on when they find a new target. Really, I should feel sorry for them; they obviously don't have anything better to do with their own lives than try to pick apart other people's.

But that doesn't mean it hurts any less.

Ryder

I GET UP LATER THAN NORMAL. IT FEELS LIKE death to drag myself out of bed, but I have a meeting with Mira later in the morning. I stick my head into Paige's room to see if she's asleep, but she's already gone, her bed neatly made. I sigh. Clearly, she's taking this job thing seriously.

She can be so dense.

I stop by her office. Given the awkwardness between us, I should've told her to sleep in. I'm pretty sure pregnant women need more rest than usual, and until her doctor looks her over and says she's all right, I don't want her to really do anything. Besides, I didn't ask her to be my assistant to actually make her work. It was just an excuse to have her back where she belongs.

"Hey, you should be taking it easy. Don't bother with…" My voice trails off when I see her face.

There are tear-trails down her cheeks, and her eyes and nose are red. She's biting her lower lip to keep it from quivering, but I'm not sure if she's aware that's what she's doing. Her gaze is focused on her laptop monitor, and her fists rest in her lap.

I stride over quickly. "Paige, are you all right?" I glance at the laptop and see a crude meme with a dead whale on a beach. It has Paige's face on it. The asshole who made it also crossed out her eyes with two *X*s. THE ONLY WAY SOME WHALES CAN DIET, says the caption.

All of a sudden there's a blood-red haze around everything I see. "What the fuck is that?"

Paige shakes her head, lower lip still caught under her teeth.

I kill the browser, nearly breaking the mouse along the way. Paige shouldn't look at such vile shit. I've had my share of disgusting lowlife haters and psychos, and I've made it a policy not to bother with social media myself for that reason. But Paige doesn't know how to deal with this kind of nastiness. Fact is, nobody should ever have to learn how to deal with it.

"What did I do that was so wrong?" It's just a whisper, her chin lowered. "Why do they think it's okay to be so mean to me?"

I kneel before her and uncurl her hands so I can hold them in mine. They're cold and clammy, but I don't care. "It's not you. It's them. They're the assholes."

She lifts her face and looks me in the eyes. "But they all hate me."

The devastation on her face twists my heart, and I hurt for her. "There are more assholes than you realize." I wipe her tears with my thumbs. "Paige, trust me, it's not you. Not at all."

"The attack outside Samantha's office...and now this..." Her head turns to the laptop.

I take her face in my hands and gently—but firmly—turn it back to me. "Paige, listen. This is not your fault. *It is not about you*. It's *their* ugliness, their smallness. And you know what? Their loss. Because when *I* look at you, I see a beautiful, smart woman who takes my breath away. And when you aren't with me, I feel like I'm missing something vital."

I'm not saying any of it to make her go ahead with our ceremony as scheduled. I mean every word, and I would gladly step between her and any ravening crowd to keep her safe and happy.

"Ryder..." she says tremulously. Her hands wrap around my wrists as she leans closer and rests her forehead against mine.

Her hair falls forward, creating a curtain around my face, and the universe tightens and contracts until there is only Paige. I kiss away her tears because that's all I can offer right now in the way of comfort. I want her to know she's not alone.

She angles her head, and her lips find mine. Everything inside me stills as I rein in an instinctive urge to deepen the connection. This is about Paige and her needs. I want her fearless and bold again. Like in the screening room before things unraveled.

She runs her tongue over the seam of my mouth, then uses her lips to relearn its shape and texture.

I adore her lips, the fullness of them, their soft fleshiness. My blood boils with a heat that has nothing to do with anger. It's all due to Paige, who is exploring my mouth to her heart's content.

Oh, the hell with it. I part my lips, and she flicks her tongue inside, letting me have a small taste. She's so damn sweet, like spun-sugar happiness and light all rolled into some kind of fabulous girl-dessert, and I crave more. I drive my tongue into her to take it.

A throaty moan vibrates through her. She slides off her office chair so we can be at a better angle. Her lush breasts press against my chest, and my cock swells.

She lets go of my wrists and rests her hands, no longer cold and clammy, on my cheeks. The contact seems to sear my skin, and I want her hands everywhere on me, exploring, stroking, fondling and loving.

Just as I want to—

"Uh… Ahem, guys."

I jerk back and curse under my breath. *The meeting with Mira.*

Paige's face is suddenly bright red, but at least she no longer has that hurt and angry look. Her lips swollen and her eyes dilated, she looks like a woman who's been thoroughly kissed.

"Don't suppose you've had time for coffee yet," Mira says, barely containing a schoolgirl smirk.

"Ah, not yet." I stand and help Paige up. She takes her seat again.

"Well, why don't you get some? You know, take that edge off. So we can actually have a productive discussion?"

Paige is on her feet immediately. "I'll get it for y—"

"You sit back down," I say. Her eyes and nose are still red—well, more like pink now—and I don't want the kitchen staff to see her like this. Besides, I don't know if it's good for her to be on her feet too much anyway. "I'll get it."

She sits, and I push her chair at the desk. "And relax. That's an order."

༺༻

Paige

Ryder goes for the coffee, leaving Mira and me alone in the room. "Nice to have you back," she says.

Her dark hair, cut Cleopatra style, is exceptionally glossy under the light, and she's wearing a black dress with a patent leather belt cinched tight around her waist. Her stilettos look long and sharp enough to kill a crocodile, with golden edging at the tips of the heels. The red lipstick is stark against her milky skin.

"Thanks," I say. It seems kind of inadequate after the display she just saw. But she and I aren't close enough to chit-chat about that kind of personal stuff.

"So I take it the wedding's on?"

"If he can give me the answer I asked for, yes."

Her dark brows pinch together into a sharp V. She takes a seat in front of my desk. "What answer?"

"It's…kind of personal."

"Okay. But this 'answer' determines whether or not you're going to show up for your wedding?"

"Something like that."

"You're kidding."

"No."

She gives me a very, very penetrating look. "Is this some kind of test?"

"Not at all."

"Then why the hell were you kissing him like you want him for brunch? You playing a game?"

"Not a game. Something very important to me."

She levels an absolutely flat stare at me. "More important than your precious friend Renni?"

"What?"

"Let me spell it out for you. Not marrying Ryder would involve consequences for her."

My chest tightens. "Are you threatening to fire her?"

"Oh, sure. I could do that, but so what? She wouldn't be any worse off than before I took her on."

Not even close to true. Everyone would know Renni was let go because Mira didn't believe she had what it took to become a star. It would be incredibly damaging to my friend.

The agent studies her manicure. "I have something better. I know her boyfriend isn't all that into her."

I lean forward. "What are you talking about?"

"Don't play dumb, Paige. He's gay. Gay men don't dig their *girl*friends."

Damn it. How did she find out? "Who told you something that ridiculous?" I ask, doing my best to stay calm and collected.

"It's called research. I make it a priority to look into my clients to make sure there aren't any surprises that can derail my efforts. She's 'dating' darling Pyotr for money so he can trick his grandfather into believing he's heterosexual." Mira tsks. "I heard that the old man really hates gay guys."

"That's crazy."

"Is it? I think you know better." She crosses her legs, the motion indolent. "I don't want to hurt Renni anymore than you do, I'm sure. I'm hoping to make her a star and make some money off her. But Ryder is my priority, and I won't hesitate to do whatever I have to make sure *you* don't do anything that can damage his image or reputation. You've already done enough with that sex tape and the scene in front of Jones & Jones."

Her blatant victim-blaming pisses me off, especially after what I put up with this morning. My voice comes out louder and sharper than normal. "I didn't release the damn tape! And I certainly didn't ask to be attacked!"

Mira almost yawns. "My dear, it doesn't matter what you did. What matters is how it affects Ryder. Besides, you can't deny that you left him. Breaking off the wedding at this point would be damaging. Very difficult to spin. You're supposed to be acting grateful to be his bride."

I'm shaking so hard, I can't speak. There are so many things I want to say, but none of them are appropriate.

"Don't think I won't use what I have on your friend to keep you in line. It's not the first time I've had to protect Ryder from some woman who didn't know her place." She stands up. "Now, in case you weren't aware, he and I have an appointment to talk about his next project. So I'm going to walk out of here, and you're going to toe the line. Have a productive day, Paige."

THIRTEEN

Paige

Mira might've left, but the after-effects of her threat haven't. My hands are shaking.

But I get up, pace a bit and take a few breaths. Try to put the unpleasantness behind me. There's work to do. Having Ryder's ring on my finger doesn't mean I get to slack off, even if he did tell me to "relax."

There are piles and piles of things to go through, and the temp assistant didn't organize any of it with any discernible logic. *Okay*, I think, surveying the carnage, *electronic stuff first*. I answer all the emails that have been read but are languishing in the inbox, then forward all the invoices to Ryder's accountant for review and payment. Next, I go back and reconcile all the weekly financial reports from said accountant with my own records to make sure everything matches up. It's one of the things I'm supposed to do, and it helps us check everyone's work to make sure that all invoices are paid on time, and there are no unusual items. Of course, since the temp assistant didn't do any of the reconciliation, I spend most of that time working on past reports.

A couple of hours later, Ryder stops by my office. I hear the clacking of Mira's heels receding down the hall.

He's still in a white button-down shirt and khaki shorts, and hasn't bothered with shoes. A day's worth of beard covers his jaw. The look is singularly disconcerting. I've seen him unshaven before, but never when it was okay to touch, and right now he looks eminently touchable. I'm also certain he won't object if I finish what we started earlier. I hide my hands underneath the desk and curl my fingers.

"You all right?" he asks.

"Fine." I smile for his benefit, although I'm not okay. Not really.

He shifts his weight. "That's a lot of stuff."

"Yeah. The temp kind of got behind."

A snort. "Did he do anything?"

"Something, I would imagine."

Ryder shakes his head. "Worthless. No wonder Mira was bitching about him."

Tension returns to my shoulders and neck. I feel the muscles there knotting up, but make a conscious effort to relax.

"What's wrong?" he asks.

"Nothing." Her threats are about me, and I don't want to involve him. Mira is his agent, and she's been with him longer than me. I don't want to cause any friction between the two of them.

He shakes his head. "You remember that question you asked me yesterday?"

The sudden change of topic disconcerts me for a moment. "What about it?"

"Do you think 'nothing' is the answer you would've given your fiancé?"

I lean back in my seat. He has a point, but I don't want to blur personal and professional. I look back at him, my mouth stubbornly closed.

"Okay." He nods as though he's reading my thoughts. "If you really considered me your fiancé, would you have said the same thing?"

"Ryder…" I link my hands together and rest them on my lap. "I'd never say a word about it to anyone, fiancé or not. It's just not my style. I've never talked about work issues to people outside the office, ever."

"Right. So. Let's try this again." He takes a seat across from me. It's the same chair Mira took when she threatened me in that gratingly languid tone. His ankle rests on his knee. "I'm also your boss. That means 'inside the office,' right? So now, tell me what's wrong."

I have to laugh. "If I ran to you every time there was a problem, you would've fired me a long time ago."

His eyes narrow. "So you aren't going to tell me at all?"

"No."

All he can do is instruct Mira to back off. And the thing is, I can sort of understand why she felt the need to show her claws. She wants to make sure I don't do anything to screw up all the hard work she's put in on Ryder. Hollywood isn't just about a pretty face and a hard body. There's an image to maintain. Ryder's done his best to be a sexy playboy, and it's Mira who's made sure he gets publicity for things other than wild parties—all the charities he sponsors and the crazy amount of money he donates to his sister's foundations. He's probably fed half the continent of Africa by now.

"Ryder, look. I can't ask you to interfere on my behalf every time I have an issue. That wouldn't be right. Also, I'm here as your assistant, not your fiancée. We should keep our personal and professional boundaries, you know…intact."

"But you'll ask me for help if you can't take care of something yourself, right?"

I've never asked him for a favor on behalf of a friend, and I don't think I can now, despite the situation. Still, I don't want to upset him. So I give him the answer he wants. "Sure."

He studies my face for a long moment. "Okay." He gets up. "Got it."

Ryder

Paige is a terrible liar. She wouldn't ask me for help if she were hiking through the Sahara with a thimbleful of water.

I thought the connection we shared in the morning meant something, but I see that it only meant something to me. It doesn't to her…not the way I want it to.

I walk back to my office. The wet bar has a fresh bottle of scotch, compliments of some new distillery. Never tried their stuff before, but I won't turn down a chance to maybe discover a new favorite.

After pouring a generous amount into a tumbler, I plop down on my usual barcalounger. I went over to see about taking her out for lunch. Yeah yeah, the media is awful, but I can get a private room at one of my cousin's restaurants without a reservation. And a change of scenery might cheer her up.

But instead, I'm more convinced than ever that unless I figure out what Paige meant by how I trust her as my assistant but not as my fiancée, our wedding may just be called off.

Seriously though, no matter how long and hard I think about it, I feel like she's overreacting. I don't think I've treated her differently because her status has changed. As a matter of fact, I treated her with more respect and consideration as my fiancée. And I loved her body like I've never loved anything before. My cock hardens every time I think about the way she tastes…or that keening sound she makes in the back of her throat when she's close to orgasm…

Shifting, I lean back and stare at the near-empty canvas that is *Beautiful Emptiness*. What few lines it has are fluid and beautiful. Mira thought I was insane to pay so much for the painting. Ditto for my business manager, Brian Miller.

Of course they share that opinion because they don't appreciate art. They only see it as an asset: buy it low and sell it high.

My mind wanders, and I start to see shapes in the blank spaces between the lines.

Lace. Smiles. That shy look in her eyes as she lowers her eyelashes. Her belly grows. Masculine and feminine hands link together. Hips bump into each other, and there's passion, but there's also more.

A genuine emotion that I can't identify.

For it to be called love, it's too damn happy and stable, like it's something that can last. In my experience, love is complicated and doesn't last. Not to mention, it comes with more terms and conditions than a mini-series contract. Break any of them, and you're screwed. There are no re-takes.

But I want what I see in the blankness. And a part of me is furious because I was so close to having it with Paige until the sex tape incident.

I could've had it all.

Now I don't know if I'll ever have it again, and the thought shreds my soul like a raptor's claw.

FOURTEEN

Paige

Ryder doesn't join me and Elizabeth for lunch. I wonder what's going on; it isn't like him to skip a meal. Elizabeth merely shrugs. "He's probably googling his name and admiring himself. The news about him paying for the animal shelters in North Carolina got out."

I shake my head. "Poor Ryder. He wants so much to keep it quiet, but not a lot of his philanthropic work stays secret, even when he tries to do it anonymously."

"Well, people are interested in what he does. Besides, I think somebody's leaking it."

I gasp. The notion never crossed my mind. "Who would do that?"

"Whoever wants Ryder to look good? For all I know, he may be doing it himself."

"No way." I frown. "That isn't like him. He doesn't like the spotlight."

Elizabeth's eyebrows almost hit her hairline. "Are we talking about the same person? Ryder Pryce-Reed?"

"I mean the, you know, positive heartwarming kind of attention. He just wants to be seen as this wild, bad playboy."

"Never going to happen. Not when he does stuff like this." Elizabeth finishes the last bite of her sandwich. "It's pretty smart actually. It creates a certain quality about him."

"Like what?"

Elizabeth considers. "Hmmm. Let's call it…an unobtainable perfection. A man who's just waiting for the right woman, the one who'll make him want to commit. I bet that's one of the biggest reasons women go nuts over him. They can't decide if he's a bad boy or a redeemable sweetheart with a gooey center."

I laugh. "You make him sound like one of those jelly-filled donuts."

She gives me a mock-serious look. "Hey now. Anything jelly-filled is redeemable."

The rest of the afternoon is filled with more work and getting caught up. Keeping myself busy has an advantage—it's impossible to dwell on stuff I can't do anything about.

Ryder does join us for dinner, and we decide

to eat at the smaller, more intimate table in the sunroom. It's like an atrium that is made entirely of glass and faces the garden. The chef sets a platter of thinly sliced roast beef wrapped around veggie sticks and alfalfa sprouts, then drizzles a special dressing all over it. There's also a basket of freshly baked bread, various cheeses, and a pitcher of fresh fruit punch.

My mouth waters at the incredible smells, and we dig in.

The meal goes well. We don't talk about what happened earlier in my office. Of course, it'd be hard to do that with Elizabeth there, but I'm grateful anyway. I really don't want to tell him what Mira said.

Ryder drapes a hand over the back of my chair, and I feel the heat radiating from it on my neck. The tension from the day melts, and I relax into the conversation.

He's in a fine mood. Elizabeth eggs him on to tell her inside stuff about the movies he's made.

"You sure?" he asks, waggling his eyebrows. "You're going to be totally disillusioned."

"Surprise me. I'll take my chances."

I chuckle. "While you're at it, surprise me as well."

Clearing his throat, he leans forward and assumes a conspiratorial air. "Okay. How about this: Most people think doing a romantic scene is pretty awesome, especially when the characters are gazing into each other's eyes and all that."

I blink at him. This is the last thing I expected him to talk about.

"They *are* really romantic," Elizabeth says.

"Well, yeah…unless your costar keeps farting."

I choke on my drink. Elizabeth snorts a laugh. "You're lying!"

"I'm not kidding." He raises a hand, palm out. "Scout's honor." The other one, the one that's resting on the back of my chair, takes a section of my hair and wraps it around a finger.

My heart skitters a bit. "So what did you guys do?" I ask, doing my best to ignore the effect his hand has on me. "Edit out the farting noise?" *For god's sake, it's just hair.*

"We couldn't because we couldn't stop laughing. Besides, she was so embarrassed it wasn't possible to continue."

"What made her so…gassy?" Elizabeth asks.

"Bean burritos and yogurt off the local roach coach."

"Oh god."

"Yeah. So not only did we get the sound effects, but that movie was done in smellovision. We had to postpone the scene for a week. That poor woman."

We all burst out laughing. Elizabeth wipes her tears. "I have no idea if it's true or not, but you better not tell anybody. People will start going through your filmography, trying to figure out who this woman is."

"Don't worry. I haven't told a soul. Besides, her agent made everyone sign an NDA afterward. He was horrified."

"If you signed a nondisclosure agreement, why are you telling us the story?" I ask.

He looks at me. "Because I have faith that you won't repeat it."

And for some insane reason, my insides turn all gooey and soft. I can't remember why I thought it was a good idea to make him tell me why he could trust me as his assistant but not as his fiancée. Maybe he already knows at some basic level, even though he can't articulate it.

"I swear I won't tell," I whisper.

"Neither will I." Elizabeth blinks away the rest of the wetness from her eyes. "My god, you'll never give me a penny if I do."

Ryder snorts, but even the joking mention of what Ryder could possibly hold over her makes my gut tighten, reminding me of Mira's threat.

"We should watch a movie or something," Elizabeth says, stretching. "I bet you have stuff that isn't in the theaters yet."

Ryder's lips twitch. "I might possibly."

"Oh come on. Isn't your latest in post-production? Don't you have a copy?"

"I do, actually."

"So let's watch that one."

He hesitates. "It's, ah, pretty violent." His gaze falls to my belly. "Totally not appropriate for babies, even if they're still in the oven."

I laugh. "I think it's fine. It's probably too young to hear anything."

Bright fire lights in his eyes as he regards me, and my breath catches. It's as sexual as any look he gave me when we made love, but there's a complexity to it as well. Like he's longing for something so bad it physically pains him.

And I feel like I'm the cause of that pain, and I want to pull him into my arms and promise to give him everything he needs so he won't feel like that again. Of course that's crazy. It's not just his emotions at stake, but mine too. What I thought would be a simple and convenient arrangement is twisting me around until I'm not sure *what* I'm feeling anymore. All I know is that I'm in way *way* over my head, and if I'm not careful there may be damage I won't be able to undo.

Not willing to dwell on my fears anymore, I paste on a smile. "Come on. Let's watch it."

Ryder

As a rule, I hate watching my own movies. It's awkward to see myself up there, doing things that most people would never do for entertainment.

The screening room is built for comfort and has a recently upgraded surround system. The furniture inside is oversized, like we're in a land of giants. I got the inspiration after staying at the Ritz one time in Thailand. Everything in that place looks like it was designed for elephants.

Paige hesitates, but takes the center couch, the one where we shared a pizza and made love, whispering our fantasies to each other. My blood sizzles at the memory, but I do my best to hide my reaction. Paige is skittish. I don't have to be particularly sensitive to know that. And I want her to relax and laugh like she did in the sunroom. Her laugh is the reason why I agreed to watch the movie in the first place.

I sit next to her on the same couch. It's so big that six more people could fit in as well. But my sister takes another one to our right. She gives me a "you owe me" look, and I answer that with a "how big of a check do you want?" look.

The movie is all slick action, with some sizzle thrown in with a hot new actress from Portugal.

It'll never get me nominated for an Oscar, but it's great for sheer escapist fun, and I liked making it.

As the movie goes on, Paige relaxes. She gasps and laughs and yells, "No way!" when the bad guy escapes about halfway into the story despite my most valiant on-screen efforts.

I roll her hair around my finger and breathe in her sweet scent. As much as I like Mira, I want to kill her for showing up when she did and ruining the moment in the office.

Paige leans closer, and soon enough she's cuddling by my side, her legs folded under her in that double-jointed way women have. I put my arm around her back. Her soft curves fit me perfectly, and I start wanting more than a cuddle. I skim my hand over her bare arm. She shivers, but doesn't move away. Desire simmers in my blood, and I want to hold her and make her come the way she did before in this room. I want her legs spread, her pussy glistening, and I want to hear her scream my name and rake her nails down my back as she falls apart over and over again. I want to remind her of the kind of sharp pleasure I can give her, how much she belongs with me so she won't ever shut me out again.

Up on screen, I get shot. A crimson blossom appears on my shirt, and the visual reminds me of Paige's bleeding.

A small jolt runs through me. We can't do anything more than cuddle right now. We still don't know what caused the bleeding, and the last thing I want is to jeopardize her pregnancy. She's already suffered so much because of me. Those memes...I've seen my share of ugliness, but they still stunned me.

But the counter-attack has started. I already called the editor-in-chief at *Lifestyle* and told him in no uncertain terms that the attacks against Paige, even if left by the users of the site, will be taken personally and I will never allow their magazine near me or my family again. I don't have enough influence to keep my family away from *Lifestyle* to be honest, but the threat was enough to make the guy jump. He swore to me that what they did was against the site's terms of service and that all their accounts will be banned immediately and the hateful comments scrubbed.

I make a mental note to talk to my team about how best to deal with the problem. I'm not having her cry again because of the assholes of the world.

FIFTEEN

Paige

I get up late. I don't know if it's the emotional exhaustion from yesterday or staying up later than I would've liked, but I don't hear the alarm go off.

When my eyes finally open, it's already nine thirty. But for some reason the room's still really dark. Frowning, I pull the curtain back and see flat, gray clouds and sheets of rain coming down hard.

I shower and put on a conservative navy blue top and a pink skirt. Since it's going to be wet, I put on boots. I need to hurry if I'm to make my appointment with Dr. Silverman.

"Damn. Look at that," Ryder mutters, shaking his head, watching the weather out the window. He lowers his hand into a small bowl of shelled walnuts. A t-shirt that says *I Heart My Life* wraps around his big, muscular torso, and he's in dark jeans and boots.

"Just a little rain," I say, grabbing a green smoothie from the chef, who offers it with a smile.

"A little my ass. It's like Noah and a bunch of animals are going to be floating by any minute." He actually looks worried. "Maybe we should reschedule," he says. "Or ask Dr. Silverman to stop by."

I take a sip of the smoothie. It's amazingly good, with a hint of mint giving it a refreshing aftertaste. "Ryder, didn't you ever learn to drive in the rain?"

He shakes his head. "I'm a man of many talents, but not that one."

"I see. Well, then, I'll do it. I'm not bothered by a little water." I start drinking the smoothie faster.

He growls. "But do we trust the idiots on the road?"

"Don't be mean," I tease. "I got mad skills."

He snorts, then chuckles. "Maybe you do."

"Come on. We're going to be late." I put the empty cup on the counter and start toward the foyer.

The housekeeper has already set out umbrellas. I take a bright pink one, while Ryder chooses black.

We take the Mercedes. It's the one Ryder insisted that I drive during my shopping spree with Josephine. The pricey car was there to ensure that people didn't gossip about me. Back then I thought he was being overly image conscious, but now I appreciate it, especially with Bethany having to take my car. It's also a very solid vehicle, more protection against wet-weather LA drivers.

And sure enough, the Los Angeleans are driving like the road is frozen solid. It's just some wetness, but they can't seem to relax. Cars inch forward, then brake, inch forward, then brake like three-legged turtles in a race.

"This is the only time I really miss Sweet Hope," I say, resting a hand on the wheel.

"When it rains?"

"Well… I miss Mom and Simon, but not the town itself." I hesitate, then add, "It has too many gossips, you know? Nothing better to do than get in other people's business. And all those 'friends' who just can't wait to be the first to tell you something bad."

Ryder nods. A moment later he asks, "How come you always call your stepdad Simon?"

"Well, that's his name. And he isn't really my dad."

"You miss your biological father?"

The question makes me pause. "Yeah. I do."

"When did he pass away?" Ryder's voice is sympathetic.

"Before I was born. We never even got to meet." I let out a self-conscious laugh. "It's so silly to miss a man who never even held me. But... he was my dad, you know? I feel like my childhood would've been different if he hadn't died in a car wreck. Mom told me he was a good man, and wanted the best for me. Growing up without him was hard, but knowing that he was watching over me like a guardian angel helped." I sniff, then scratch the tip of my nose. "Pretty stupid, huh?"

"No." Ryder reaches over and squeezes my hand.

I let him keep holding it. The connection feels fragile yet so precious.

If I just throw caution to the wind... Could this turn into something more?

I'd like to believe it. My lips still tingle when I think about the way he comforted me in my office yesterday. And I loved the way he held me in the theater room last night, his breath tickling my neck and his hand on my arm, skin to skin.

Elliot asked me why having Ryder's trust mattered when we were only marrying for a year. Maybe it's because I'm afraid. Afraid that if I'm not careful, I'm going to fall in love with a man who doesn't have that high a regard for me.

Ryder is the only man who affects me like this. And it started even before we began talking about the marriage. He can drive me crazy, irritate me until I want to kick him, but then he makes me laugh just as easily or turns my insides soft with his sweet gestures. And when he looks at me these days, it's as though I'm the only woman for him, as if all the other women before me have crumbled like pillars of salt and blown away in the winds of his memory.

And his kisses heal the wounds left by the ugly comments better than anything.

I turn my hand so I can squeeze him back. He pulls it to his mouth and kisses the knuckles.

"What's that about?" I ask.

The smile he gives me is so brilliant, my heart flutters. "Just because."

Ryder

The first word that pops into my head when we step into Dr. Silverman's office is "soothing." The sage green and creamy yellow colors are remarkably calming. Instead of posters about dangers of this or that disease, the walls have prints of modern art.

I approve. If the doctor is as good as the office décor, the concierge fee I'm paying for the clinic will be money well spent.

The receptionist leads us into the private area where we can see the doctor right away. In her forties, Dr. Silverman is skinny. Her appearance isn't remarkable, short with an average face and mouse-brown hair. Her outfit is also predictable—a white lab coat over a conservative coral tunic and black skirt.

Lines around her warm green eyes crinkle when she smiles. Paige relaxes, and right then and there, I decide I like the good doctor.

She gives us a friendly nod. "Paige. Mr. Reed."

"Call me Ryder," I say. Mr. Reed is what people call Dad.

"Of course." She gives me a polite smile and turns to some charts.

I appreciate the professionalism. After the intros, she doesn't spare a single extra glance my way. Her focus is entirely on Paige and the baby.

"If you don't mind, let's see what's going on."

There is some drawing of blood, a bunch of scans. The doctor checks Paige's ankles and hands and feet, making notes.

I wait, feeling superfluous. Dr. Silverman is thorough and obviously knows her business. Finally, Paige lies on a bed and arranges her clothes to reveal her belly.

"Come closer." Dr. Silverman gestures at me. "We're going to look at the baby. Don't you want to see?"

I swallow. I came with Paige for moral support, but didn't expect to see the baby. She hasn't shown me a single ultrasound image.

I drag my ass over and position myself so I can hold Paige's hand and look at the black and white monitor. The doctor spreads some kind of gel over Paige's stomach and runs a wand over it.

At first I don't see anything except some white lines and dots all over the monitor. I'm not sure which one of them is supposed to be the baby. Then the image settles into a black hole and a tiny bean-shaped dot inside it.

"Isn't it sweet?" Dr. Silverman says. "That's your baby. It's fine and healthy in there as far as I can see."

I blink. That tiny life is the reason why Paige agreed to marry me in the first place. It was the cause for both of our scares when she bled.

The doctor measures the baby and makes notes on how far along it is. It seems impossible that she can do that with something that small inside Paige, but well… I guess that's medical science for you.

"Everything's on track. I don't see anything to worry about. Six weeks and five days. Perfect. Let's see if we can hear the heart beat." Soon I can hear loud and rapid *whoosh-whoosh-whooshe*s.

"What is that?" I ask, while Paige's jaw slowly slackens.

"Your baby's heartbeat." Dr. Silverman looks at the measurement. "Let's see… One sixteen per minute."

"It's so…fast," I say in awe. Paige's hand tightens around mine.

"It's actually pretty normal."

"Wow." I run my hand over my face and realize I'm shaking. Some emotion I can't identify rises up in my chest until I feel like my sternum is going to crack. Seeing the little bean and hearing its heartbeat makes the baby feel so real. It's no longer just an abstract concept growing inside Paige. It's so much more, and I'm at a loss to describe the wonder of it.

Dr. Silverman tries, but she can't quite hide the smile that's threatening to come out. "Congratulations. The baby is healthy."

"Then why did I bleed?" Paige asks.

"Sometimes that happens, but it doesn't necessarily mean you're having a miscarriage. Of course, we should take extra precautions, and I want to see you again next week. Also, I strongly urge you to not overexert yourself. Get plenty of rest and avoid stress as much as possible. I understand you have a wedding coming up, a 'once in a lifetime' event, but so is your baby. Delegate as much as you can." Then she gives me a look. "I expect you to make sure that happens."

"Yes, ma'am," I answer meekly.

We thank the doctor and leave. I have Paige sit in the waiting room, while I talk to the receptionist about the next appointment. The young woman is nowhere near as professional or cool as Dr. Silverman. She's virtually fucking me with her eyes.

I let it roll past. Other women are no longer my concern. They can look all they want, but right now the only person I care about is Paige.

As the receptionist hands me an envelope with the print-out of the ultrasound and a card with the information about the next appointment, I hear a loud gasp behind me.

"No!" Paige cries. She's looking at her phone, her face drained of blood.

I shove the envelope in my pocket and take a few big strides toward her. "What is it?"

"Bethany." Paige's eyes are wide, and her face is so pale I'm afraid she's going to pass out. "She's been in a car wreck."

SIXTEEN

Paige

I MANAGE TO CALM MY NERVES AND DRIVE TO the hospital address Oliver has texted me. If the roads weren't wet, Ryder would probably take over, but…

If it had been anybody but Bethany, I would've assumed the weather had something to do with the accident. But she's not a California native, and she's a great driver, even in snow.

Ryder puts on shades and an old cap as I park the car. Renni and Gary are already in the waiting room by the time we make it inside. Oliver's usually smiling face is devoid of color, and his narrow shoulders are hunched almost level with his ears. The rimless glasses sit skewed on his nose, but he doesn't seem to notice.

I run over to him. "Bethany?"

"The doctors are with her right now," Oliver says.

"What happened?"

"The police think somebody ran her off the road." He drops his hands. "There were skid marks. But they aren't telling us anything more."

"How about the other driver?"

"Didn't stop."

Anger laces through my worry. I know some people are horrible about stopping and doing the right thing, but this is just awful. Ryder puts a hand on my shoulder and squeezes. I lean toward him, grateful for his support. My knees are unsteady, and I can't help but imagine the worst.

"The baby?" I manage to ask.

"I don't know." Oliver wipes tears away. "There was blood on her, Paige. So much blood." He covers his face with shaking hands.

My vision dims. Bethany and Oliver tried so long and hard for that baby. If anybody deserves one, it's—

"Paige!" Ryder's urgent voice rings in my ear. His arms are tight around me.

I blink a few times until my eyes focus. Ryder's peering at me, his brows scrunched.

"What?" I ask, my voice low.

"You went limp, and I thought you fainted."

Maybe I did faint for a moment. I have no idea. I find a seat and try to collect myself.

Ryder watches my every move. Eventually he turns back to Oliver and the others. "Is there anything we can do to help?"

Oliver shakes his head and sighs. "I doubt it. You should go home. I didn't mean for all of you to come. I have no idea what I was thinking."

I stand up—gingerly—and walk over to hug him. "You did the right thing. You deserve our support." Gary and Renni nod.

I don't know if Oliver can hear me though. His gaze is focused on something beyond us, and his mouth is tight with denial. I recall the terror I felt when I was brought to the hospital, bleeding, and I wasn't going through the trauma of an accident on top of it. He and Bethany must be petrified. What if the unthinkable happens…?

Ryder checks his phone and texts for a moment. He probably needs to cancel whatever appointments he has for the afternoon. I realize that even though I'm supposed to be his assistant again, I don't know what he has scheduled for the day.

Finally he gets up. I put a hand on his forearm. "Don't go," I say.

"I'm not leaving. Just need to check on something."

"Let me come along." I don't want to be alone with my dark thoughts. Renni and Gary don't seem to know what to do either, Gary staring at nothing and Renni tapping her feet two hundred beats per minute—her little tick when she's tense and worried. It seems like Ryder is our only steady anchor, and I need that.

He debates a moment, then nods. "Okay. Come on."

We take an elevator to the top floor. He leads me down a hall until we reach a section marked PRIVATE, which of course means nothing to Ryder. He pushes the door open and walks in. A secretary in a regular street outfit of a blouse and slacks looks up. "Do you have an appointment?"

"No, but I'm pretty sure Rob Sanders will see me, assuming he's available," Ryder says, taking off his cap and sunglasses.

The woman's eyes go wide with recognition. "Oh my god... Um, of course. Right this way."

She takes us to a small conference room with a view of the parking lot. I look out onto gray, wet concrete and spot our Mercedes.

Within minutes, an enormous man walks in. Thicker than an old oak, he's in a short-sleeve button-down shirt and black slacks that are held up by suspenders. His thick red beard covers a big portion of face, and freckles cover the rest. Other than the beard, he has no hair on his head.

"Good to see you, Ryder."

Ryder shakes hands with him.

"And your beautiful fiancée. So lovely to meet you. I'm Rob, director of this fine hospital." His big hand closes around me. He is surprisingly gentle and careful, a man very much aware of his own strength.

We all sit down at the table. "So. What can I do for you?" He winces apologetically. "Normally I'd spend more time on preliminaries, but I have an appointment in fifteen minutes."

"It's about a patient who just came in. Car wreck."

"This damn weather," Rob mutters, glancing at the rain outside.

"She's pregnant," Ryder says. "I have no idea what her insurance is going to cover, but I want you to do everything in your power to make sure she's okay. If there's a procedure that can increase the odds by even half a percent, I want you to do it. Don't worry about the cost. I'll cover it."

I jerk my head his way, but Rob has already produced a pen and scrap of paper from some pocket or other.

"What's the name?"

"Bethany…" Ryder glances at me.

"Uh, Smith. Bethany Smith," I say. "Her husband's in the waiting room. His name is Oliver."

"Okay." Rob jots both names down. "I'll take charge of her care myself."

"Appreciate it," Ryder says.

"No problem. Tell your mother I said hello."

"Will do."

We exchange goodbyes and leave. Ryder puts his cap and sunglasses back on.

"Thank you," I whisper as we take the elevator back to the first level.

"No problem." He links his fingers with mine. "Bethany shouldn't have to…" He swallows, then clears his throat. "Money shouldn't come between her and the care she needs."

I rest my head against his shoulder. He speaks as though it's the most obvious thing, but not every person can be so open and generous. I've seen people in his social circles who are so tight-fisted they could make a penny squeak. "Don't say it's nothing. It means everything to Bethany and Oliver. And to me. Thank you. Thank you. Thank you."

∞

Ryder

WE WAIT UNTIL A DOCTOR COMES OUT AND TELLS us that Paige's sister is stable for the moment. Even so, she can't go home yet because they want to make sure she's really out of danger, especially since she's pregnant. He wants to limit her "excitement" and says only Oliver can see her.

Oliver tells us to go home and rest for a bit. It isn't until then that I realize we've been at the hospital for close to five hours, and none of us have eaten.

Paige's friends, Renni and Gary, had to leave earlier to go to work. She texts them both to update them.

By the time Paige and I finally exit the hospital, the rain's stopped. The roads are a patchwork of wet and dry spots. I put a hand on her shoulder.

"I'll drive," I say, pulling out my keys. "We should stop by a restaurant on the way and get you fed."

She blinks at me. "Food?" Like it's a foreign concept.

"Food." I open the door for her. "Gotta keep your strength up."

That stubborn look comes into her eyes, but I shake my head. "Nuh-uh. You're pregnant, too, Paige. Neglecting yourself isn't going to help Bethany."

Suddenly the fight goes out of her, and her shoulders slump. "You're right." She slides into her seat.

I close the door and get behind the wheel, thinking, *Well, that was easy enou—*

"I really don't want to go to a restaurant though," she says. "Can we just eat at home?"

"Sure. Let's call the housekeeper."

The drive back is somber. Silence hangs heavily, but neither of us breaks it. I'm aware of her breathing, the way she's looking out the window without seeing anything. It's as though the happy glow from the visit with Dr. Silverman vanished, just like that, and only an ashen dullness remains.

The chef has prepared grilled cheese sandwiches with salad, and it's all probably delicious. At least the texture's nice, but I can't taste anything even though I'm forcing myself to take hearty bites. I suspect Paige is the same from the way she nibbles at the corners of her sandwich. A sparrow would be taking in more calories.

"Paige, come on," I say. "Eat."

"Sorry. I just…don't have any appetite." She puts the food down, resting her elbows on the table and buries her face in her hands. "It feels wrong to eat now."

"Bethany wouldn't want you to skip meals."

"I know, but…" She sighs. "It's like, I'm okay, and my baby's okay, and she and her baby are maybe not okay. And between the two of us, the fact is, she's the one who deserves a baby more."

Her voice carries sorrow and an odd thread of self-recrimination, and my heart aches for her. "What is this, a competition?" I say, trying to lighten the mood. "You both deserve good things.

You both deserve to be happy and fulfilled. Just like every expectant mother."

"But Bethany and Oliver have tried so hard to have a child. They're married, and stable, and can provide the best of everything. So why me? I'm pregnant with my ex's baby, who by the way is such a jerk that he secretly filmed us having sex and then put it up for all the world to see. I'm using you so I won't be a poor single mom, and so you're forced to go to the doctor's appointment to…" She shakes her head. "God, we were at Dr. Silverman's office, looking at my baby, hearing its heart beat, while Bethany…Bethany…" She chokes and stops. "Excuse me." She jumps to her feet and runs upstairs.

I sit for a moment, wanting to give in to tiredness. Then I push my chair back and level myself out of it. *Nope. Nuh-uh.* Not going to let her get wound up like this. Not going to give those toxic emotions a chance to fester.

I go after her.

SEVENTEEN

Paige

I run into my suite and shut the door behind me. Tears scald my cheeks, and I press a fist against my mouth to muffle the sound. Once I get myself slightly under control, I slip off my rain boots, put them in the closet, and then just sort of stop, wondering what to do.

I know Ryder is right about my stepsister and me both deserving good things in life. But I'm also right. Bethany is the one who can provide a better life for a baby. Every statistic and study I've read says she has all the pieces in place to raise a child successfully. And I don't.

It makes the world seem hopeless, and I start crying again.

Ryder walks in without knocking. He plucks a few Kleenexes and hands them to me. I wipe my eyes and stand there, apparently unable to do anything but weep.

He pulls me closer and sits on the edge of the bed. "Paige, don't. You're going to make yourself sick."

"I'm fine," I croak.

"Then why are you crying like this?"

I shake my head since, of course, I can't answer him and I'm not really fine.

"Just listen to me, okay?" He rocks me gently without waiting for a response. "Do you really think your baby deserves a lesser chance than Bethany's because you aren't married or I'm not the father or…whatever?" He shakes his head. "You have no idea how much I wanted that baby when we were at the doctor's and I heard its heartbeat. Who the father is wasn't even on my mind. The only thing that matters is that it's your baby—a part of you. That is more than enough for me to want it."

A lump bigger than both of my fists combined lodges in my throat, and I can't breathe through the hot emotions swirling in my heart.

"Being related to someone biologically doesn't guarantee you'll be a good parent," he continues, tightening his hold on me. "Just look at my folks. They're so busy with their lives and making snide jabs at each other that they don't care about us at all…except when we can be used to make a point.

You're going to be an awesome mom, Paige, and your baby deserves the best, just like every other baby in the world."

My lower lip trembles. My gaze is wet as I lift my face to look at him. "You shouldn't say stuff like that." *If you keep on like this, I may fall in love with you, irrevocably and forever.*

"I know." The smile he gives me is rueful, like he's reading my unspoken thoughts. "But I've never wanted to say the words before. I never felt what I felt back in that doctor's office, Paige."

Something breaks loose inside me. This man, outwardly perfect and wonderful, inwardly flawed and struggling and all too human…this exhilarating, exasperating man who could have anyone and is wanted by everyone…this man is saying the sweetest thing anybody has ever said to me, and he's saying it like it's the most obvious sentiment in the world. He has faults—and issues—and he may be letting his past destroy his future, but he's really trying to connect with me despite it all.

His words burn through my fears and worries until all I know is that he has my heart. He's had it for a while now. I just didn't want to admit it because I knew our relationship would end a year after we exchanged wedding vows.

Why am I wasting what little time I have with him? Demanding explanations is an exercise in stupidity. Assistant, fiancée...who the hell cares? I should cherish every moment we have together and make as many good memories as possible before it ends...because that's all I'll have of him.

I lean forward and kiss him. My mouth is clumsy, and my hands are shaky with emotion, but I have to taste him right now.

He hesitates as I move my lips over him. But it doesn't take long before he parts his own and pulls me to him. And even though it's only our lips touching, it's so intimate and sweet it makes my heart pulse with longing.

We continue kissing until I'm light-headed with want and something more...and with every second that passes, our kiss deepens until I don't think we can ever untangle our mouths. Every cell in my body is fully attuned to Ryder. I sense his every shudder, every contraction of his muscles, the way he holds me, as though I might vanish if he isn't careful. Liquid heat spreads through me; my whole body feels as if it's bubbling and melting, like sugar over fire.

He slowly runs his hand down my back until he reaches the end of my navy blue top. His fingers move underneath, and he gently caresses my bare skin. "You're so soft," he whispers.

His gaze focuses on me, and I lean back slightly to pull my top over my head. I want him to see me exactly the way I am because I know I'm beautiful in his eyes.

He lays me back on the bed and sighs softly as he looks me over, his face etched with admiration. He kisses me again, then drags his mouth along my jaw, his lips as light as a butterfly on a flower. They travel down my neck, and he licks the particularly sensitive spot over my collarbone until I'm quivering. I'm already soaked, and he hasn't even touched my breasts.

He dips his head until he can bury his face between my cleavage. The sight of his dark head against my pale skin is intoxicating. We haven't been together in a while, and I want him inside me *now*—even though at the same time I want to prolong this as much as possible.

His hand moves up, cups a breast, bra and all. When he turns his head to the other one, I shrug until the bra strap falls and the cup pulls away. He kisses the underside, his breath tickling my nipple until it hardens. I move my legs restlessly. "Please," I beg, shoving my hand into his hair and guiding him toward where I want him the most.

He goes without any resistance, pulling the tip of my breast into his mouth. I cry out at a pleasure so sharp it almost hurts. He scrapes his teeth along the soft flesh, then traps the nipple between the roof of his mouth and tongue and sucks, his cheeks hollowing.

I buck, my hips leaving the matress. "Ryder…" I sob out. My nipple's never been this sensitive, and desire has tightened its grip to where I can barely breathe.

He merely hums in response. The vibration travels all the way to my clit, and I squeeze my eyes shut at the most exquisite sensation. I arch my back, silently begging for more.

And he obliges.

He is relentless, a conqueror on a mission. It's not just his tongue, but his teeth, lips, beard stubble…everything working together to drive me insane. He doesn't neglect my other breast, making sure to massage it, priming it. To anchor myself, I dig my hands into the mattress, each arm tight and straight by my side. The position also arches my back and pushes my tits forward, but I don't care as long as he keeps going.

When he finally lets my nipple go with a pop, I can barely think, my body is so close to shattering. He undoes the front clasp on my bra and pushes it out of the way.

"You're so fucking hot," he says. "Beautiful." His hand glides down my torso, then he yanks my skirt and panties off in a sudden motion, making me gasp. "Wet." He cups my soaked pussy and groans. "Mine." He then takes his glistening fingers to his mouth and licks. "Sweet."

He's still wearing clothes. I lick my lips. "Get naked," I say.

He stands, smiling slightly. "Come help me."

My eyes narrowed, I get up. My knees are a little wobbly from the pleasure singing through my veins, but I manage to keep my balance. Besides, I know he's going to catch me if I fall.

I push his shirt over his head, revealing the gorgeous, rippling muscles. Hair sprinkles his thick pectorals. I place a hand over his heart and feel it thundering a hundred miles an hour despite his cocky smile. I let my fingers glide lower. Every square inch of his stomach is defined, not an ounce of fat anywhere. "Your abs should be framed and hung on a wall," I murmur.

"Nobody would be able to afford it." Despite his light tone, there is need coloring his voice.

As I reach lower to unbuckle his pants, he plays with my nipples and squeezes my ass. My blood is back to boiling, and I give him a stern look. "If you do that, I can't focus."

"Never said I'd let you focus," he whispers hotly against my neck.

I shiver. My concentration is shot, and he knows it. He lowers himself until he can take my other nipple into his mouth and suck.

My mind spins away. Another layer of syrupy pleasure settles over me, and I don't even care that now my inner thighs are slick as well. He settles me back on the bed. The suction of his mouth suddenly increases, and he runs one long finger along the wet flesh below, then circles my clit.

I scream as a sudden orgasm jolts through me like lightning. He gives me a wicked grin. "That sensitive, huh?"

I pant. When I can get enough air to speak, I say, "Pregnant women tend to be more responsive."

The grin widens. "Oh *really?* This is going to be even more fun than I thought." He glides down my body, stroking my breasts tenderly. "Now I can eat you up like I've been thinking about," he murmurs, "make you come over and over again."

He spreads my thighs, his hands gentle but firm. He takes his time, licking my inner thighs, inch by torturous inch. His tongue must be magic because everywhere it touches, I feel nothing but searing desire. It's as though he's branding me as his.

When he finally takes my clit in his mouth, I'm so close that I clench my hands to keep from climaxing. "You can come again," he whispers, uncurling my hands. "You can come as many times as you want." Our hands link as he dips his head back down…

…and I let go.

He isn't finished. His glorious, greedy mouth keeps sending thunderclaps of pleasure through my body. My spine bows until it feels like it's going to break, but he is merciless. I no longer know the number of times I've screamed his name. After a while, I can't even do that because my brain is fried.

When he finally untangles our hands, I'm a puddle of spent flesh. The mansion could collapse on us right now, and I wouldn't care.

Ryder gets rid of the rest of his clothes with remarkable economy and returns to bed. His cock is thick and hard, its head almost touching his belly. He positions himself between my legs until the tip is pushing slightly into my dripping, swollen pussy.

His mouth is back on mine, his kiss savage but no less sweet. "My god, I love—"

My heart stops for a moment. *Is he…?*

A quick pause, then he continues, "I love what you do to me. I love what I can do to you. I love the way you lose yourself with pleasure with me." His whispered words fan against my ear.

A small thread of disappointment knots around my heart. Of course he wasn't about to say, "I love you."

But when he cradles my face between his big, strong hands and pushes into me, while looking into my eyes, disappointment is the furthest thing from my mind. Bone-deep pleasure begins to crest, each thrust pushing me closer and closer to the peak.

The connection I feel with him leaves me breathless. My heart swells with emotion, and tears leak from the corners of my eyes. But still, I don't look away. I spread my legs wider and welcome him into me.

When the orgasms barrel through both of us, we cry out and hold on tight, as though afraid of losing each other in a tempest sea.

EIGHTEEN

Ryder

I clasp Paige's naked body tightly to mine. Having her like this feels so right. This, right here, is exactly how we should be.

Her beautiful lips curve into a satisfied smile. Euphoria surges through me, knowing I'm the one who put it on her face.

I press my forehead against hers and breathe in her scent. My heart is still drumming, and I'm relieved I didn't slip up.

I love you.

Where did that come from? It just popped into my head, rolling out of my mouth as I kissed her.

It's better that I say nothing. I doubt she would've gazed back into my eyes and told me, "I love you, too." Paige is smart and practical. She would never do something as unproductive as falling in love with a guy she'll ditch in a year. Being with me hasn't been easy for her, and she wouldn't be bothering if it weren't for what I can offer for her baby.

As I let my hand wander over her curves, I remember the ugly things people said about her and how hurt she was. I never want to see her shed tears over a bunch of assholes' comments again. After a beat of hesitation, I say, "Paige, do you want to go overseas?"

Sleep weighs her voice until it's languid and mellow. "You mean for the honeymoon?"

"No. Until the wedding. It might be good for us to get away from all this…pressure."

She shifts until she can look me in the eyes. "I thought you wanted to put on a good show for everyone?"

"We don't have to be here for that. Besides, I'm tired of being hounded… Aren't you?"

"Oh god, yes. But…I worry about Bethany." Small lines form around her eyes and mouth. "I can't leave town until I know she's okay."

"Of course." Paige is too sweet to abandon her stepsister, even if leaving might give her some peace.

"We can talk about it later when we're sure she's going to be okay. But do you really want to go overseas now? We have so little time before the wedding."

I pull her closer. "That's why I hired a team to handle it. So we don't have to worry over every detail. Like I said, all we have to do is show up and say our vows." I try to keep my voice light, but somehow I can't. The one-year period starts the moment we say, "I do."

She snuggles against my chest and falls asleep. Her breaths tickle the spot over my heart. I study her face. Her long lashes fan over her cheeks, and her nose wrinkles as she rounds her mouth and mutters something that I can't quite catch.

I don't break the deals I sign. Despite my wild-boy reputation, I take my career seriously, which is why directors and studios love me. Only idiots think they can be high maintenance divas and have a long, flourishing career in a town as competitive as Hollywood.

But a horrific urge to rip up the prenup and tell Paige she can leave when I'm dead and buried pulses through my veins. Instead, I lie back and stare at the dark ceiling until the sound of her soft breathing lulls me into a restless sleep.

Paige

Ryder's gone by the time I wake up. Maybe he couldn't rest well and just gave up. I felt him toss and turn a few times during the night, but I was so tired that I faded back to sleep just as quickly as I was jostled out of it.

The room is meticulously clean, all my clothes neatly folded and placed on a chair. Did Ryder do that? *If so, he might actually be ill*, I think, laughing to myself.

The bedside clock reads nine. I stretch lazily and grunt at the satisfying soreness between my legs. I check the phone. A text from Oliver is waiting for me.

All OK. Thank god. But Bethany is being kept for observation. Just in case.

My body sags in relief. I write him back: *Glad to hear that. Can I see her today?*

A few moments later, he responds, *Sure*.

"Yes!" Pumping my fist, I hop out of bed. Bethany is going to be fine. Her baby's undoubtedly all right as well, or Oliver would've said something.

I want to see her ASAP, make sure everything's really okay. Then I'll talk to Ryder about possibly going overseas. It might be a good idea for us to get away from the spotlight and spend some time together without any pressure. Come to think of it, we've never really had a chance to spend any time together alone.

After a quick shower, I throw on a bright magenta t-shirt dress that says "High on Life" in snazzy diagonal teal green letters. By the time I reach the kitchen, Elizabeth and Ryder have finished breakfast, although they're lingering over coffee. She looks like she's ready to model for some glossy fashion magazine. Her hair is perfectly curled and gathered into a bouncy ponytail, and the dress she has on matches the shade of red on her lips. Ryder's more casual in a gray Avengers t-shirt and shorts.

"Good morning," I say.

"Morning." Ryder pulls me to his side before I can move past him and gives me a quick kiss on the mouth. He hasn't shaved, and the hair on his jaw scrapes my skin deliciously.

Elizabeth raises an eyebrow, but a smile tugs at her mouth. "The chef saved you an omelet."

On cue, a plate of omelet shows up along with utensils and a thick cloth napkin. I sit and start eating. It's fluffy, with three of my favorite cheeses. The housekeeper places a glass of OJ beside the plate, for which I thank her quietly.

"I just heard from Oliver." I turn to Elizabeth to bring her up to speed. "My sister got into a car accident yesterday."

"Oh no! I hope she's all right."

"What did he say?" Ryder asks.

"She's fine. I can go see her today." Thankfully the weather's nice, so I won't have to deal with people acting like the world is coming to an end on the highways. "I was thinking about going after breakfast."

"I'll go with you."

"Don't you have a meeting?"

"It can wait. This is more important."

I smile at him. "Thank you."

Ryder squeezes my shoulder and kisses the spot behind my earlobe. The affectionate gesture makes me flush, but I'd lying if I said I wasn't happy.

He glances at his buzzing phone. I lean over, curious. Not ten people in the world have that number.

"Don't be nosy," he scolds, though his voice lacks any heat. "I gotta take this."

He disappears upstairs.

"So," Elizabeth says in a stage whisper. "You guys make up?"

"I guess so."

"I'm glad." She smiles, resting her chin in her hand. "You're so perfect together. It's obvious you have feelings for each other."

"You really think so?"

"Uh-huh. Ryder obviously adores you, and way you look at him…well, I know that look."

My jaw slackens. Since I just realized I love him, her observation about me isn't entirely wrong, but…*Ryder?*

He loves what we do for each other in bed. I guess that's a feeling of sort, but not the kind she's talking about. If Elizabeth thinks he adores me, it's only because that's what he wants her to believe.

After all, he is a very talented actor.

"Did I say something?" Elizabeth peers at me.

"No." I force a quick smile. "I was just thinking about Bethany."

She nods, but it's obvious she doesn't buy it. "Give him a chance, Paige. I know it's hard to believe a playboy like him can be sincere, but he's not a bad guy. Not in his heart, where it counts. And I'm not saying that just because he's my brother."

"I know," I say quickly.

Her gaze remains skeptical, and I'm sure she doesn't understand why I'm reacting like this to her observations. The thing is, I don't want Ryder to know how I really feel about him. Countless women before me have told him they loved him, and he always responds with a rueful combination of pity and resignation. I don't think I could stand it, to see that look on his face and know that, this time, it was directed at me.

I already know his heart is off-limits for me. The least I should be able to do is keep my pride.

Ryder

I shut the door in my office before calling the detective. Benjamin Clark is on retainer with Mom's side of the family, and he is eminently trustworthy. I texted him yesterday to figure out what's going on.

"Benjamin," I say. "It's Ryder."

"Thanks for getting back to me. Your instincts were right."

Icy fear knots my gut. I found the circumstances of Bethany's accident strange. She grew up in Idaho just like Paige. There was no reason for her to be driven off the road, unless the other driver was driving too fast and didn't bother to hit the brakes.

"The victim was driving an Altima, which is registered to your fiancée. According to my source within the police, the other car didn't slow down at all. Unless the brakes just weren't working, it was deliberate."

"Fuck." I sit down, my legs unsteady. *Bethany was driving Paige's car?* Then the target was probably Paige, not Bethany.

"Are you aware that your fiancée has quite a few …detractors? I saw at least three comments on social media about wanting to put her in her proper place, and I wasn't even trying to find anything in particular about her." Benjamin harrumphs. "Normally I would chalk it up to idiotic people being loud-mouthed, but given what happened to her sister…"

"Damn it. Damnit, damnit, damnit." I shove a hand into my hair and tug until it hurts. It's all my fault. I should've known she might become a target. Haven't I been harassed by some truly deranged "fans"? What would stop them from transferring some of their obsession from me to Paige?

I let my pride, my needs, trump common sense. I wanted to show Dad I wouldn't make myself miserable to fulfill the conditions of getting Grandpa's portrait of me. The revenge couldn't just be me getting the painting, but showing the world, especially Dad, I'm having a grand fucking time doing it. I told Paige I wanted the wedding of the century, all the publicity and the kind of glitzy show that would leave people breathless as they watched our fairytale marriage unfold for a year.

Why the hell didn't I stop to think how it would impact Paige?

No, not just Paige. The people she cares about, too.

If she'd known agreeing to marry me for a year would jeopardize her stepsister and her baby, she would never have done it.

"Oh, one other thing," Benjamin says.

"What is it?"

"My man at the police department also said there was a nurse who tried to attack you at a hospital some days ago...?"

"Yeah. Typical wack-job fan. What about her?"

"She was bailed out. The woman threatened to take you away from your fiancée using whatever means available. At that time, the authorities just assumed she was ranting, but given the circumstances, they are trying to locate her. Just in case. It's better to dot all your *i*s and cross all your *t*s, especially when it concerns a member of a family that's always been generous with the department."

"They *let her out?* I told them she was a psycho, and that she was likely to come after me again. I specifically asked them to keep her in jail as long as they could until the trial...or at least notify me if she got out on bail or something."

"Mm. About that... The DA has decided not to prosecute."

This is starting to sound like something out of Kafka. "Why the hell not? The woman *bit* me, for god's sake!"

"I agree it's strange. And I can't quite figure out what's going on, because there are elements of the situation that don't really add up. For example..."

Benjamin pauses, and my gut twists until I taste acid in the back of my mouth.

"...apparently, it was you who told them to drop the charges."

NINETEEN

Ryder

My hand tightens around my phone until my knuckles are white. "What the *fuck?*"

"I knew you would say something like that."

"No, seriously. What the fuck?" I repeat. "Me? Let her out? There's no way."

"I'm inclined to agree, but my source told me it's true, and he isn't the type to make mistakes on things like this."

I press my thumb against the spot between my eyebrows. There are two people in the world who can act as my representative. Mira and my lawyer.

But neither of them received any instructions about the nurse. There wasn't any reason, since the DA was handling it.

"Did your buddy say anything else?" I ask.

"No. But I suggest you talk to your people."

"Oh, you can count on that," I say grimly.

I end the call and am about to dial my lawyer when Paige knocks on the door and sticks her head in. "Ryder, you ready to go?"

You go ahead, something came up is on the tip of my tongue, but I swallow the words. I promised to go with her to the hospital, and I do want to see how Bethany's doing. It's a hundred percent obvious now that her being hurt is my fault, and I need to make sure she and her baby are all right.

I ask Paige to drive since I can't do that and text at the same time. I send a quick question to my accountant.

"Are you all right?" Paige asks. "If it's something I can do, just let me know and I'll deal with it." She gives me a small sideways smile. "Probably be faster that way."

Pain knots behind the spot where my forehead meets my eyebrows. This is one thing I can't delegate to Paige. If she finds out, she'll rip up our prenup and tell me to go to hell.

"Nah, it's nothing," I say, flashing her Reassuring Look Number Four. "Don't worry about it."

Paige

Now I know something is wrong. Ryder's insouciantly confident glance is one I recognize from his movies, but have never seen him use in real life. It's too practiced, too…perfect.

However, I also recognize the stubborn set of his jaw. He's not going to tell me anything right now.

So I keep my eyes on the road and think. I've never seen him not delegate tasks. If he could, he'd delegate eating and sleeping.

His phone rests next to his thigh. Who was he texting? And about what?

Anthony.

The name slips into my mind. I scowl. What could he and Ryder possibly have to say to each other now? He knows what my leaving his condo for Ryder means, and he told me that hurting me didn't give him the satisfaction he wanted.

But he also said that didn't mean he was going to stop.

Okay, true enough. But he seems too sensible to pursue something that won't give him anything in return. At least, I hope so.

I breathe deeply. I shouldn't drive myself crazy with whatever private business Ryder has. It won't do me any good, and right now, my priority needs to be making sure Bethany and her baby are all right. Once that's done, I can take the time to talk to Ryder about going overseas and…anything else.

Even with so little time before the wedding, it's probably a good idea to go somewhere away from the paparazzi and media circus. Try to unplug and pretend that none of the craziness is happening.

The hospital looks brighter and nicer on a sunny day. I park the car, and Ryder, cap and sunglasses in place, comes around to open my door and help me climb out.

We reach Bethany's room and peek around the corner. It's private, and large enough that it has a couch that can be used to sleep on. Oliver is seated on it, thumbing through a magazine. I take a quick glance at Ryder and mouth, *thank you*. The hospital wouldn't normally have given her this level of treatment.

Bethany's asleep, her face toward the window, away from the door. I make sure to be as quiet as possible so we don't wake her up.

Oliver notices us and gets up. He hugs me, then shakes hands with Ryder. My brother-in-law's shoulders look even narrower than normal, his usually round face slackened into a gaunt oval. Dark circles show under his eyes.

"Did you get any sleep?" I whisper.

He gives me a smile. "Some." He nods at Ryder. "Thank you for the upgrade."

Ryder shrugs, shuffling a little. "It's nothing. The hospital people here like me."

Wrapping my arm around his waist, I give him a quick squeeze. It's so sweet to see him uncomfortable about his generosity. If it had been a strip show, he'd be relaxed and bragging about how he paid top dollar for the girls with the best assets.

Bethany murmurs something, then turns to face us. I can't help it; I actually gasp at the sight.

She looks like she's been in a boxing match… and lost. Red gashes run across her swollen forehead, cheeks and the bridge of her nose. Ugly yellowish-purple blotches discolor her left temple and jaw.

"Should've seen me yesterday," she jokes, her voice raspy. "I'm actually looking pretty hot this morning."

"Oh my god…" My hands shake.

"Don't. I'm feeling okay." She looks over my shoulder at Ryder standing behind me. "Hey, Ryder." She gives him a quick smile like he's just some guy, rather than one of the most famous actors in the world, which is of course what makes her so awesome.

"Bethany," he says, his gaze somber. "How are you, really?"

"I'm going to be rich if I get a dollar every time somebody asks me that. I'm doing fine." She sits up, and Oliver jumps to rearrange the pillows so they support her back. "I had another exam this morning. Everything's okay, nothing's broken, and the baby"—her hand rests over her belly—"is doing great. We heard its heartbeat. Strong, loud and fast."

Oliver kisses the crown of her head. "The doctors think we're okay, but they said to let them know immediately if we notice anything even remotely abnormal about her condition. Just to be on the safe side."

"My worry right now is my comic schedule—"

"*Bethany!*" I can't believe she's thinking about work!

"—and the contract."

"I'll handle it," I say.

"Huh?"

"I said I'll deal with it. You need to get well and not worry about comics or contracts or…anything like that."

"Thanks, but I can take care of all that," Oliver says.

I cross my arms. "No, you need to be with your wife, making sure that she and the baby are fine. I'm good at handling details like this. Trust me."

"Well…I hate to involve you, but it isn't that complicated," Bethany says. "There're just some notes that need to be taken to my lawyer. I didn't get to type them up before, you know…"

"No problem. I can do that."

Bethany has the neatest handwriting I've ever seen. Her lawyer won't have any problem understanding what she wants. And if he needs clarification, he can always call her.

"Well, okay. If you insist. They're on my desk in my office." She smiles. "And thanks."

Ryder

It's pretty obvious that Paige wants to take care of the contract stuff for Bethany as soon as possible. Since I'd also like some time alone to figure out who's pretending to represent me, I tell her to take the car and go. I'll arrange for a ride later.

"Are you sure?" she asks.

"Positive. I know you're going to worry about it otherwise, and the traffic's not too bad right now." Not that that's saying much. It is L.A. after all.

"Okay. Thanks." She goes on tiptoe and kisses me on the mouth. The spontaneous public display surprises me. She's never done it before. Warmth curls in my belly. I hug her tightly, wanting to prolong the moment.

"Catch you later." She gives me a quick smile and slides into the Mercedes.

I watch her leave, then pull out my phone when the car disappears from sight. The lawyer's office has already responded.

Lex is on vacation. Will be back next week. If urgent, we can have one of his associates take a look, but it may take longer.

Of all the time to be on vacation, naturally it has to be today. The other people in his office aren't as familiar with my situation…but I don't feel like waiting.

Yes. Have somebody else get me the answer. It's urgent.

I also text Mira, but she's out of town as well for some emergency meeting with production people for one of her clients. I consider calling and asking her point blank, but something stops me. It'd be better to see her reaction in person when we talk about this. *Can you swing by as soon as you're back in town?* I text.

Will do.

The sight of Bethany's face won't leave me. She looked awful, and I bet there were a lot more bruises and injuries underneath the hospital gown. The woman is admirably upbeat, but I wish she'd at least groused about how unfair it was that she's hurt or something. That might've made me feel…

I narrow my eyes. *Less guilty?* The realization doesn't make me particularly proud of myself.

If someone on my team caused Bethany's accident—directly or indirectly—I have to take care of it. And without involving Paige. Keeping her in the dark is lying by omission, but the alternative is losing her.

And I can't lose her. Not now.

TWENTY

Paige

Even with the lighter than normal traffic, it takes a little over an hour to reach Bethany and Oliver's house. My phone's been buzzing nonstop in my purse, but I've been ignoring it. I never talk on the phone when I'm driving, not even for Ryder.

After I park the Mercedes in front of the house, I check the log. I have like a gazillion unread texts and over twenty missed calls.

All from a number I do not recognize.

I frown. My number isn't exactly a state secret, not the way Ryder's is, but it isn't public either. Since there are way too many texts for me to read—most of them repeating *Call me back. It's really urgent!*—I dial. There is a possibility that it's some freak who managed to get a hold of my mobile info, but it could also be somebody who genuinely has pressing business…

It takes only two rings before the other party answers. "Thank god you called me back!"

Every cell in my body tenses. "Shaun?"

"I've tried to call you for days, but you wouldn't answer."

"I had your number blocked, obviously! Do you honestly think I want to talk to you?" Then something else occurs to me. "Are you stalking me? I'm pretty sure I'm not supposed to talk to you after what you pulled."

"Okay, okay, *don't hang up!*"

"Go to h—"

"Paige, I didn't do it! I swear!"

Anger and something far uglier churn in my heart like a dark, stormy sea. "Riiight. A camera just set itself up in your closet and happened to start recording when we were having sex. Then the video conveniently uploaded itself to YouTube through your computer."

"No, you don't understand! Okay, I did the recording. I thought it would be…well, you know, hot to look at it later. Besides, I thought I looked good in it."

"Oh, for god's sake! How do you ever find hats to fit your head?" I can't believe I dated this man, thinking he was the best I could do. Good lord. I'd rather sew up my lady parts than be with him ever again!

"But Paige, I swear to god, I didn't upload it anywhere! Just think for a minute. What does the tape get me? I'm not going to become famous because of it. Nobody gives a shit about the guy in those videos, you know that. *And* it would only piss off Ryder, which is *not* what I ever wanted to do. I wanted him to star in my movie!"

"Shaun, I really don't give a damn what you did because the sex video is out there for everyone to see, including my parents."

"Did they really watch it?"

"I don't know and I didn't ask," I spit.

"I can't get a gig anywhere now, and Ryder's lawyers are demanding, like, ten million dollars. What the fuck? I know he's blackballed me."

"*Good*. I told you you'd never get anywhere with him. But you're so full of yourself you wouldn't listen."

"No, *you* aren't listening. I didn't do it! I'm telling you, my account got hacked!"

"Sure."

"I'm serious. I even had to change my password."

"To what? Shaunisawesome?"

A short pause. "How did you know?"

I close my eyes. "Oh my god…" I can't even. "Shaun, listen to me very carefully. If you ever call me again, I will tell Ryder, and his lawyers will add harassment to whatever they're suing you for already. I'm not going to lift a finger on your behalf, so you've just wasted both our time. You should spend your energy trying to convince Ryder and his lawyers that you are an *innocent victim* of hacking!" Breathing hard, I hang up and toss the phone back into my purse.

Just thinking about what he's done is infuriating. But at the same time, the fact that he's going to pay for it sends a hot streak of satisfaction through me. I told Ryder to let it go, but maybe he was right to teach Shaun a lesson. Some people just won't learn without getting their wrists slapped, and I have a feeling that Shaun is one of the slower ones.

I climb out of the car and unlock Bethany's house. Her office is on the second floor, so I climb the stairs and find it tidy as usual. She absolutely abhors clutter. I see a stack of papers on the desk plus a spiral notebook. I open it to make sure it has notes for the contract. Satisfied, I put it in my purse then stop. The first page of the contract has the information about Bethany's web comic site and the other party: The Reed Trust.

I pause for a moment, remembering Julian's threat. He wanted me to humiliate Ryder by ditching him at the altar. If I wouldn't cooperate, he was going to start going after the people I care about. Is this somehow part of that threat?

I scan the contact info further. An address in L.A. Then a name: Brian Miller.

I blink. Brian Miller is Ryder's business manager. Brian has other clients, of course, but this…

And there have to be other Brian Millers in Los Angeles, I tell myself. It's not an uncommon name.

Still…

I tap my finger on the paper. If Ryder had created a trust, he probably wouldn't have named it "Reed" since he hates Julian and everything his father stands for. On the other hand, he did adore his grandfather. And he genuinely enjoyed Bethany's comics. So he could've formed a trust and named it "Reed" for his grandfather, then decided to fund Bethany's comics.

I skim the rest of the paperwork, looking for clues. All I come away with is a sense that Ryder is not behind it. If he were, the contract terms wouldn't be so onerous. He would've been tough, of course, but much fairer. He wouldn't be asking to hold Bethany's comics hostage for twenty-five years in the event that the partnership breaks up, and he certainly wouldn't be demanding that Bethany match at least fifty percent of the money the trust is pouring into the venture.

But first things first. I take the notes and go back to my car, locking the house back up on the way out.

The drive over to Bethany's lawyer's office isn't bad. The receptionist is a friendly Asian woman in her late fifties. Steel gray streaks her otherwise jet black hair, and she has large gold earrings in the shape of musical notes. "Thank you," she says, taking the notebook. Her face creases as she smiles.

"Mind if I ask you a question?"

"Not at all."

"Do you know who owns The Reed Trust?"

"Hmm. Not really. Let me see." She taps a few keys on her laptop. "Nothing here except a contact number for the representative. Brian Miller. Do you need his information?"

"Could I get that number from you?"

"Sure." She writes it down and gives me the slip of paper with another smile.

Sure enough, it's a number I recognize. As I leave the office, I call Brian.

"Hallo, Paige." His voice is lightly accented—British I think. He always sounds jovial and cheery. "I'm surprised to hear from you. Thought you'd be busy with the wedding."

"Not quite that busy. We have a good team in place to help."

"Always pleasant to hear. What can I do for you?"

"I wanted to know about The Reed Trust."

"Ah." Something in his tone changes. I can almost imagine him shifting his weight in his seat. "Of course, I can't go into detail. Attorney-client privilege and all that. But it's a fairly complex trust. Multiple layers."

"Is it Ryder's?"

"No, I wouldn't imagine so. It belongs to a client one of my colleagues used to handle, but after his retirement, the account came to me. I've yet to meet the client, actually. Just his lawyers."

"I see. Apparently, it's interested in funding my stepsister's web comic business. Bethany Smith?"

"Ah. That. A good opportunity, I thought. She's quite talented."

"Thank you."

We exchange a few pleasantries and hang up. What he says makes sense. If it were Ryder's, he would know.

But… I shake my head. *Reed.* It's just too big a coincidence.

Then I tell myself to stop being paranoid. Still… I can't ignore the bad feeling. I dial Gary, who picks it up after a few rings.

"Sup, Paige?" he says.

"I wanted to know if you can help me with something." Gary's a natural extrovert, and knows all sorts of people.

"Shoot."

"You said one of your friends is a PI, right?

"Yeah. He mostly does boring stuff like following spouses around town, seeing if they're cheating or not…although he's also pretty good at digging up hidden assets during divorce proceedings." Suddenly he stops. "Uh…you need something like that?"

I chuckle. "Ryder isn't cheating on me, so no."

"Okay. Whew."

"It's about a trust. I want to know who owns it, but I can't seem to find the info."

"I can ask, but it's gonna cost you. That guy *never* works for free."

"I can pay." One thing about living with Ryder, my account has been growing fatter because I don't have to spend any money on food or clothes or…anything, really. "I'll text you the info. Tell him it's urgent."

"Okay. I'll make sure he gets on it ASAP."

"Thanks." I hang up. I'm probably going to end up wasting that money, but I'd rather be safe than sorry.

TWENTY-ONE

Paige

IT'S BEEN TWO DAYS SINCE RYDER AND I VISITED Bethany in the hospital. I watch my phone like a hawk, but there's nothing from Gary or his friend. Bethany is back home and seems to be doing well. Her face is slowly returning to normal, and she's back on top of her contract negotiations, which are apparently becoming a pain in the nether region. But she's managing.

Ryder is another matter.

He makes love to me at night as desperately and passionately as before—that time when I thought he was going to say, "I love you." But during the day, he's distant, often in deep in thought, and paces around his office, his hands curled into fists. He doesn't even glance at the scripts Mira sends over, and it isn't like him to neglect work. If I didn't know better, I'd say he was worried.

I want to figure out what's wrong, but every time I ask, he turns it aside with a joke. I'm not imagining things though; even Elizabeth notices.

"He is acting a bit odd, isn't he?" she says over late morning coffee.

I nibble on a cracker. "Yeah. Did he say anything to you?"

"Nope. Nothing. I'm almost worried about him."

"Why?"

"He was like this when we heard that our grandpa was ill. The doctor wasn't sure if he would recover, but grandpa eventually pulled through."

"Anyone in your family sick?" I ask.

"Nah. All of us siblings are a sturdy lot, and he certainly wouldn't act like this if it was Dad."

I frown, unsure what to make of Elizabeth's revelation. After we finish our mid-morning snack, I go to his office. Sure enough, Ryder's pacing again.

"Hey." I put a hand over his fist.

"Huh?" He stops pacing and looks at me, blinking as though he's having a hard time switching gears.

"Are you still worried about Bethany and her

baby?" Normally I wouldn't assume that, but he did show unusual concern for their welfare…

He doesn't answer.

"They're doing fine, okay? And it's thanks to the excellent care she got at the hospital, which was largely due to your talk with Rob."

Ryder's lips part, then he looks away.

I'm not letting him ignore that. I put a hand on his cheek and guide his face back until we make eye contact. "I saw Bethany yesterday. She's glowing…despite the bruises. She'll be fine. The baby'll be fine."

"I know."

And he believes it. It's in his eyes. But his voice is off. It isn't the usual light, flirty tone or the occasional serious, decisive tone. It's wavering between fear and indecision. "Then what's wrong?"

"It's… I just have a lot on my mind, that's all."

"Is it because Elliot's trying to marry a stripper?" That's the only thing I can think of.

Now he really looks at me. "How did you know that?"

"He told me. He came by Bethany's place when I was staying there. He wanted to explain that nothing happened at the club, and that the only reason you guys were at the strip joint is because he was looking for a bride."

"Is that why you eventually decided to come back?"

"No." He asked me why Ryder's trust mattered so much to me even though we're only marrying for a year. I wasn't able to answer him, but now I wonder if my subconscious already knew I was in love with Ryder. "It was…something else."

Ryder nods. "Okay. Well, it's not about him. I knew about his plans, and, you know, whatever. I don't care if he wants to marry some glorified hooker."

My mouth hangs open. "The idea doesn't bother you at all?"

"He has his reasons for doing things, and he can be quite the rebel. He doesn't have to worry about a public image, and he hates doing things just because other people tell him to. Not to mention he has more money than he knows what to do with. So…no, it doesn't. He can go ahead and do whatever he wants."

"Wow."

A smile ghosts over Ryder's lips. "Yeah. 'Wow' is most people's reaction to Elliot."

I grin at him, wrapping my arms around his torso. I don't know what to tell him to make whatever he's worried about go away. But I'll offer what comfort I can.

He rests his chin lightly on the top of my head and squeezes me back.

"Thank you," he whispers after a moment.

"For what?"

"For being with me. And for being you."

We stay like that together for I don't know how long until my phone goes off. I pull away reluctantly.

It's a text from Oliver. *The police caught the other driver.*

Who? I type and hit send.

Some psycho fan of Ryder's. Apparently she's been stalking and sending him gifts and stuff. Actually she was arrested not too long ago for trying to assault him at a hospital.

That doesn't make any sense. *Why would a stalker try to hurt Bethany?*

She thought it was you in the car. Bethany was in your Altima. Didn't we tell you?

No, I start to type, my fingers numb and clumsy, then stop. He might've told me, but I might've not heard. I was beside myself with worry and the worst-case scenario at the hospital. I delete *No* and respond, *Maybe. Don't remember.*

If we didn't, sorry. I called the insurance when I knew Bethany was going to be okay, and they've been in touch with us to get more info, etc.

No, no, I'm so sorry. I'm so sorry. It's all my fault. I should've thought of the possibility before I let her take my car.

Oliver's reply is instant. *Do NOT blame yourself, Paige. It's not your fault. You're not responsible for other people's actions.*

I close my eyes. If I hadn't let her drive my car, she wouldn't have been run off the road. No, my car has nothing to do with any of this. It's all because people see a bull's-eye painted on my back.

Now the name Reed on the contract from the investor for Bethany's company is feeling less and less coincidental. What if it's something more nefarious? After all, people I love are getting hurt…because of me.

"Paige? You okay?" Ryder asks, peering at my face.

"The driver who ran Bethany off the road. They caught her."

"Her?" His voice is much too cautious.

"One of your stalker fans. A really dedicated one, who got arrested not too long ago for trying to get to you at a hospital."

Both of his eyebrows rise, but not before his face turns white and his Adam's apple bobs.

"Did you know?" I ask.

He shoves his hands into his pockets. "I wondered when I heard that Bethany was driving your Altima and that the 'fan' was out of jail."

"Is that why you've been acting so odd the last two days?"

Two beats, then he says, "Partly, yes."

"I see. I…wish you'd told me."

"I wasn't sure."

I drop my head. "I hate this, Ryder. I really do."

"Paige…"

"I let her borrow my car because hers was having trouble. No big deal, right? For most people, it's not a big deal."

"You're right. It's not a big deal."

"But it became one." Tears prickle my eyes. "I can't even do something nice for my stepsister without getting her hurt, and all because I'm…" I stop to take a shuddering breath. "I don't even know what I am to the public. People want to hate me, fine." I slash the air with my hand. "If they want to make memes or write terrible things about me, you know, whatever. But they can't…" I press my lips until they're numb. "They can't hurt my friends and family. It's not fair."

"Paige, they won't. I won't let them."

He wraps his arms around me, and I absorb the warm comfort he's offering. "Maybe we should go overseas," I say, my words muffled. "I hate it that we're running because of…*them*. But if people know we aren't even in the country, they might leave my family alone."

"Okay. So let's go."

I tilt my head so I can look at his gorgeous face. "Where were you thinking about?"

"Not Europe. Too much press there." He frowns. "How about southeast Asia?"

"It sounds so far away."

"Well, that's the point, right? And it's not that bad."

My phone buzzes again in my hand. I look down, expecting Oliver again. But it's Gary.

The trust is actually owned by Mira Brasson's agency. I'm surprised you didn't know…isn't she Ryder's agent? Maybe she's managing it for Ryder.

I shake my head in disbelief. There is no way. Mira doesn't manage Ryder's money. He has a business manager, an investment advisor and an accountant and a bunch of other people for that, and they've done a spectacular job of multiplying his fortune. The only thing Mira manages is his showbiz career.

Then I remember how she told me she would hurt Renni if I didn't behave. Nobody can be allowed to make Ryder look bad, and that includes his "fiancée." Not only that, she made it clear she's done it before to keep women in line.

I look at Ryder. It seems unbelievable that he would ever allow Mira to go that far to protect his image. But to somebody like him, image is everything, isn't it? As grating as Mira can be at times, it's hard to imagine her doing all this without his knowledge.

And if he knows, but does nothing, that makes him complicit…doesn't it?

"What is it?" Ryder asks, his tone overly modulated. There is a tight tension about him, like he's expecting something to break any second.

I pull away from him. "Did you know Mira is managing a trust for you?"

He frowns. "No. I never heard anything like that."

"Well, she is. It's called The Reed Trust. And it invested in Bethany's comic business."

Still frowning. "That's good, right?"

"I don't know, you tell me."

He starts to take a step forward, but something on my face stops him. "Paige, I don't know anything about this trust. I thought Bethany had plans for the site but if she doesn't…"

"She threatened to hurt Renni, you know."

"Who?"

"Mira. She told me if I didn't behave and make you look good, she would release some damaging information about Renni and her boyfriend."

Ryder's face starts to change. "Okay, hold on. When did this happen?"

"The day I came back to my job," I say.

"She told you that herself?" Confirming the fact.

"Yes."

"Why didn't you say something?"

"Because I can't run to you every time I have a problem with someone who's essentially a coworker."

"But blackmail? That's more than just 'a problem.'"

"I thought maybe you knew. I didn't think she would say stuff like that without your blessing."

He jerks back like I've just slapped him. "You honestly thought I was capable of something like that?"

"Ryder…you have to understand. At the time I didn't know how far you'd go to continue with the ceremony. You told me how much your grandfather's painting means to you, and you were willing to claim a baby that isn't your own to get it."

He's looking at me like I'm some kind of incomprehensible creature, and sweat slickens my spine. I have to make him understand. "Mira also told me she's done it before. What was I supposed to think? At the time, you made it clear that without you, my baby and I would be without money or any kind of benefits."

He runs his hands over his face. The gesture muffles a sigh. "We never had a chance, did we?" Resignation leeches all power from his tone. His shoulders slump, and he looks…defeated.

"What do you mean?"

"To you, I was always just a source of money and security for your baby. And maybe some fun in bed. But I was never somebody you could lean on. Never someone you would ever go to for help because I'm just…not that kind of person to you."

Something in his tone frays my nerves. I feel like I'm about to fall apart like an old, moth-eaten sweater. "It's not like that. Ryder, we were both under enormous pressure at the time. I just didn't think it would be good for me to burden you with the news or try to create unnecessary friction."

"Mira is my *agent*. You are my *fiancée*. Can you not see which one matters more?"

"I'm a fiancée you're going to get rid of after one year. Mira will be with you forever. She managed your career since you started acting. She helped you become a big star."

"*No!*" he shouts, flinging his arms out violently. "She would *not* have stayed with me, not if she disrespected you like that! Don't you understand? Don't you get anything?"

I shake my head, sudden dread filling my heart until I'm cold from the inside out. "What am I not getting? Help me understand."

"*I'm in love with you!*"

The announcement is like a hammer falling from the sky. If he had told me that any other time, I would've been ecstatic, but this… I can't even process what's happening.

Red suffuses his face, and he's breathing hard. "And all you can think about is our damn divorce to come in a year. After all this"—he digs his fingers into his hair—"I'm not even sure why you're still with me, except maybe it's that you need money a lot more than I thought you did."

The words hit me one after another like bullets. I never knew until now how they can leave a person bleeding. "Ryder!"

He's shaking his head. "No. I just… I can't look at you right now."

Something inside me crumbles but I know I have to stop him. I have to make him see that he's mistaken. That I love him too.

But he's already moving, his hands palms out. "I have to go…before I say something I'm really going to regret."

Before I can stop him, he's gone. The door closes with a bang, leaving me alone and shaken.

TWENTY-TWO

Ryder

By the time I park my Ferrari, my head has cleared a little. I look around and realize I'm in Elliot's underground garage. How did I get here? It's as though instinct has brought me to the one person who can maybe understand what I'm going through.

Then I reconsider. Elliot won't understand anything. He's never been in love.

But at least he'll be good company. He'll let me drink and won't pester me with questions. And he certainly won't look at me with that expression of horror and shock that came over Paige's face when I told her I loved her.

It would've been a lot less painful if she'd just stabbed me with a knife. An electric, double-bladed carving knife. Serrated, like they use on turkeys at Thanksgiving.

Set on high.

Thankfully, Elliot is home when I buzz his unit on the top floor. He looks like shit though. His hair is sticking up everywhere, and he has a least two days' growth of beard. He's in a white undershirt and pale gray shorts.

"What are you doing here?" He rubs sleep from bleary eyes. "What time is it?"

He stands aside so I can walk in. At least the penthouse is clean. Stacks of magazines lie neatly in a rustic basket, one he brought back from Tuscany a couple years ago. The glass tabletop is dust-free, the white couches are spotless, and the hardwood floor has a fresh coat of wax. There's even a vase full of fresh daisies on the dining table.

Not that any of it is due to him, of course. Elliot is a complete pig who couldn't figure out how to turn on a vacuum cleaner if you taped the switch to a stripper's nipple. His housekeeper comes by four times a week to keep the place neat. Otherwise the government would seize it for health code violations.

"It's late morning." I check my watch. "Actually, it's noon."

He yawns, his jaw cracking. "Yeah. Early. I didn't come home until six."

"You still hitting the strip clubs?" I sit down on

a couch and try to stretch out. My neck and lower back are tight, and it's not from working out.

"Yup." Elliot sprawls in an armchair.

"So what's taking so long? Is there a bimbo embargo or something? Just pick one and marry her."

"Can't."

"Why not? It's only for a year."

"I can't just marry *any* stripper, even if it's only for a year. Gotta make sure she's super hot."

I roll my eyes. "The clubs you frequent, they're all pretty damn hot. And again, it's only for a year. So why bother?"

He squints at me. "You're making me worried. Did something happen with you and Paige?"

"I don't want to talk about it."

"Scotch, then?"

"Yeah."

He grabs a couple of bottles and a pair of tumblers. Unlike our eminently appropriate and genteel sister, Elliot doesn't care what time it is when he feels like drinking. Sun's over the yardarm somewhere, and all that.

"I thought…" He scowls and starts over. "You know, Paige likes you."

I take a swig. The burn feels oh so good. "She likes my money. And whatever she gets because of the prenup."

"What is she getting out of the prenup?"

"More money."

"But that's okay, right? I mean, you wrote the prenup."

My tone grows testy. "Of course I wrote the prenup. I hired the lawyer."

"So what's the problem?"

"The problem is that she wants to end it after a year."

Elliot stares at me like I've just spoken to him in Mongolian. "Have you been snorting something?" he finally asks. "You're not making any sense. She is doing exactly what you want her to do. You should be thrilled. Hell, you should be cartwheeling across the city that she isn't being clingy. Any other woman would've been clutching at your pants and crying, 'No, Ryder, no! I'll do anything! Don't leave me!'" he says in a falsetto.

My teeth grind together. Maybe it was a bad idea to come here. "I don't want to end our marriage after one year."

Elliot takes another scotch. "You want to change the duration? You know you can't end it soon—"

"No! I don't want to end it! Period."

Elliot chokes on his drink. Some of it comes back up, and he covers his nose. "Shit! Ah, that's nasty." He grimaces at the wet spots on his shirt, then pulls it off completely. It ends up in a heap on the floor. "Does this mean what I think it means?"

He takes in my expression and leans back, his mouth parted in wonder. "Son of a *bitch*. You're in love with her."

"What about it?" My voice is belligerent.

He shakes his head slowly. "Oh. My. God. Who would've thought? You were complaining about how marrying her is the cliché of all clichés. What was it you said? 'Not even Hollywood would make a movie that terrible'?"

I grind my teeth so hard my jaw aches.

"I just think it's funny. You know, in a *holy shit* kind of way. Of all people, you are the *last* one I thought would fall in love. Your mom's side of the family isn't exactly known for warm, touchy-feely stuff."

They aren't, although things seem to be changing there. Even my sociopath cousin Dane is hooking up with somebody. So who knows? Maybe it's my turn.

But I'm sure if Fate is real, the bitch is laughing at my expense.

Elliot sniffs. "Look, I know the love business bothers you. But if you don't want her to leave you, why don't you just tell her you're in love with her? I'm sure she'll cry with joy and promise to be with you till death do you part. All that good st—"

"I already told her." A painful sense of loss and humiliation burns through me. "She was horrified."

Elliot's eyes bug out. "Seriously? You sure you didn't misread her emotions? I mean, you must've been nervous. Probably just didn't catch the, I don't know, subtle nuance of her expression or something."

"I was *not* nervous, you jackass. I'm never nervous around women. And I know how to read Paige. Trust me. She was absolutely, utterly horrified."

"Wow." Elliot raises his eyebrows and gazes pensively down into his whiskey. He doesn't say anything for a few moments. Then, "Sorry, man. That's just…awful."

It's worse than awful. I can't decide what hurts most. That she doesn't love me back, or that she never considered me someone she could depend on. Why can't she see that I want to provide and care for her?

"You still want to go ahead and marry her?"

"Yes. And in any case, I can't call it off now without humiliating her." I laugh bitterly. The media would bring up the fact that she starred in a sex tape, and the vultures would come out again. "But what's the point? I can't have her for a year and then lose her to someone else out there she wants more." I don't know how I ever thought I could let her go after one year. Was it because I didn't know I was in love with her?

I wish I could go back in time and somehow make sure I never realized what's in my heart. Then it would hurt less. Ignorance was indeed bliss.

"I'm sorry." Elliot brings out a third bottle of scotch. "Two won't be enough."

I nod and knock back another mouthful of fiery drink. But no matter how much alcohol I consume, I can't push Paige's horrified expression out of my mind.

This is probably why men never say, "I love you" to women first. Rejection and humiliation I can deal with. I suffered through plenty of both when I was young and starting out in Hollywood. But the idea that she will never be mine…that someday she'll leave me and find somebody else… cuts me wide open.

If it didn't affect Paige, I would rather call off the wedding than have her for a year only to lose her. If I get used to life with her—as my wife— there's no way I'm going to survive the divorce… and life without her.

Paige

RYDER DOESN'T COME HOME. I TRY CALLING, BUT

he's not answering. Elizabeth tries as well, but she only gets his voicemail.

"This isn't like him. Wonder where he is." She puts down her phone.

"No idea. He didn't tell me anything." I already checked his calendar. He doesn't have any appointments this afternoon. A moment later, my phone buzzes and I jump for it. Maybe it's Ryder calling me back.

I need to tell him I love him too, and that I never told him because I was afraid. I need to tell him that I was stunned by his declaration and that he is definitely wrong about where I was coming from and that I want him back home.

Mira's name flashes on the screen, and I deflate faster than a spiked tire. "This is Paige."

"Is Ryder there? I've been trying to get a hold of him for over an hour."

I hesitate, debating if I should confront her about her role in funding Bethany's company. A part of me wants to hash it out right now, but rationality prevails. It isn't the kind of topic I can talk about over the phone, especially when I'm emotional and unprepared. Mira is too sneaky and slick. "No. He left this morning and hasn't been back."

"He said he wanted me to swing by. Apparently he has something important to discuss."

"When did he contact you?" Ryder was so angry earlier. Maybe he wants to talk to her about the threats she's posing against my best friend and stepsister.

"A few days ago. I was out of town, but I'm now back."

Okay. So whatever he wanted to talk to her about can't be the blackmail stuff. "Well, I don't know what it's about. But I'll let him know you called when I see him."

"Great. Thanks." She hangs up.

"More people looking for him?" Elizabeth asks.

"Yeah."

"Where *could* he have gone?"

It's a rhetorical question. "Excuse me. I have to get some work done."

I go upstairs to my office. I need to make two lists. One is everything I want to tell Ryder regarding his declaration. The second is all the things I'm going to tell Mira to get her to leave me and my friends and family alone.

I'm going to fix this.

TWENTY-THREE

Ryder

Something buzzes, the sound like a large and particularly obnoxious bee.

It continues. Probably something important.

I look over at Elliot. "Visitor," he mumbles.

We've killed two bottles of scotch. The third one is about a quarter empty. Alcohol smolders pleasantly in my veins, and I don't ever want to leave Elliot's couch.

"You tell anybody you were coming over?"

"No." I glance at him. "Probably someone delivering another inflatable doll."

Elliot gives me the finger. "It's not a delivery guy. They just dump the packages at the concierge desk and run." He groans and levers himself up. "All right, all right." He mutters a few choice words, then buzzes the person in.

"Who is it?"

"Your agent."

A mix of ugly emotions rears its head. I glare at the door as Mira walks in. She's in her usual black dress and shiny black patent shoes, and she looks as slick as spilled oil. Her red lipsticked mouth purses. "Good god. What the hell is this?"

"I'll leave you two alone to talk business," Elliot says with a loopy grin. "Call if you need anything. I have plenty more scotch…some vodka too." He wags his fingers and goes into his bedroom.

She crosses her arms and stands hipshot, looking down at me. "You asked to talk to me as soon as I was back in town, and now you ignore my calls because you're too busy drinking. Not even Paige knows where you are—or maybe she just said that because she didn't want to tell me the truth."

The mention of Paige triggers something inside me. It's as though Mira's hit a detonation switch. "Don't talk about my fiancée," I grind out.

"Oh for god's sake." She throws her hands up. "What the hell has she done now?"

"You are my *agent*, not my *mother*. You should've stayed the fuck out of Bethany's business. And you should've never threatened Renni!" My voice rises. "She's your client!"

Mira's lips curl in distaste. "A client I took on so Paige would do the right thing and marry you for a year. I wouldn't have accepted her otherwise. She's pretty enough and has some talent, but she isn't that special. She won't amount to anything."

"You don't know that. Have you even tried to get her any roles?"

"No. Because it's all going to end in a year. So who cares?" Mira frowns. "Is this why you wanted to see me? To check on how much I'm doing for her?"

I start to shake my head, but it hurts. Shit. If I'd known I'd be confronting my agent, I wouldn't have drunk so much. "Did you tell the DA that I was going to let it go when I made it clear I wanted that nurse prosecuted?"

"Yes, and it's for your own good. If we go after her, people are going to start talking about why you were at the hospital—and the fact that Paige released her sex tape right around that time would never die its natural death. Do you really want that attached to your name for years?" She stalks over to the kitchen and gets a glass of water. "Here. Drink this and sober up."

I take the glass. "You've done this before, haven't you?"

"What?"

"Cleaned up after me to manage my image."

"It's part of my job. Talent has to be managed. Nurtured…cultivated. Nobody becomes a star without careful planning. And you're golden, Ryder. You're young, handsome, rich and from a good family. You're wild and bad, but you also do good things like those charities you sponsor. Problem is, young men with looks and fame tend to do stupid things, especially where women are involved."

I stare at her. Memories of how Mira and Lauren used to whisper between themselves flood through my mind. "Like Lauren," I say.

Mira looks away, but not before I catch the slight shift in her expression.

"I remember you two used to talk to each other all the time."

"Lauren." She shakes her head. "She wanted me to be her agent. Even though I told her it wasn't a good idea. My loyalty was—is—to you. And I wasn't going to ruin my reputation by shilling her to casting directors just because she was sleeping with you."

"But there was more, wasn't there? She went to every party you were invited to." Even through the alcohol, I'm not completely stupid. "What did you promise her?"

Mira shrugs. "I told her I'd introduce her to some people. And I did. Half the trick is networking."

"You mean like coke-snorting stars and wannabes?"

"I had no idea she was using. And if she was, it has nothing to do with me. I'd never condone anything like that."

Right. And I was born yesterday. "You made sure Lauren would go down a destructive path. It wouldn't be that difficult if you put your mind to it. People who are desperate to be discovered will do anything, follow any fucked up piece of advice, if they believe it'll give them an edge. And you were a big name agent even then."

"You're out of line, Ryder. I never held her down and pushed powder up her nose."

"No. You just made sure she met the wrong crowd." Pain sears through me. "But Paige can't be manipulated that way. So you chose a different method this time."

"Oh for god's sake. What does it matter?"

"It matters because the wedding's off."

Mira stares at me. "What?"

"I'm going to make an announcement."

"Seriously?" She curses. "Okay, let me see the statement before you say anything. We have to make sure you're ditching her. The tape gives us the perfect excuse."

"No, it doesn't. *She* called it off because I'm not someone she can see a long-term future with."

A breath hisses out of her. "She wouldn't dare."

"Why not? Are you going to pull the funding from her stepsister's company? Make sure to release another psycho from prison, so they can run one of her family or friends over? How about Renni? You going to make sure she pays, too?"

"None of that will happen if Paige behaves. It's only a year, Ryder."

"Why do you have something named The Reed Trust?"

"I don't know what you're talk—."

"*Don't fucking lie to me!*"

She sighs. "All right. Yes. I have a trust for each major client. It makes it easier for me to keep track of what I'm doing for them. But I've never used it for anything that could come back and reflect poorly on you."

"You're such a piece of work. If I'd known what a barracuda you are, I would've never signed with you." I take a take a deep breath, but the vise around my chest still tightens. "You have no respect for me or my personal life."

"*You have no personal life!*" She slaps her hands together in irritation. "You are a fucking superstar!"

I sit back. Of course. That's what all this is about—Mira wanting to ensure that I'm one hundred percent hers. Not in a romantic sense. She's not minded that way, plus romance requires one to have a heart. But she can ensure I'm always alone, or surrounded only by people she approves of, so that I'll always be on a path that leads me back to her.

My voice is quiet when I tell her, "Then I'll stop being a fucking superstar."

She snorts. "Don't be an idiot. You can't do that."

"Sure I can. I don't have to work to get by. I've got more money than I know what to do with." I bare my teeth. "Oh, and Mira? You're fired."

Her chest shudders, and she purses her lips so tight, countless small lines form around them. "You're drunk. Drink that water, go sober up, and when you're thinking right again we're going to pretend this talk never happened." She turns and heads toward the door.

"No, we aren't." I look at the only agent I've ever had with anger and regret. Anger wins. "If you come near me, Paige or anybody either of us cares about ever again, I'm going to slap you with a restraining order so fast it'll take your breath away. And then I'll have fun watching you try to spin that to protect *your* image."

TWENTY-FOUR

Ryder

I sober up, and for the next four days stay at Elliot's. I can't go home. Knowing that Mira is behind Lauren's drug use and Paige's stepsister almost losing her baby… Fuck. I can't forgive myself for not seeing it sooner.

I should've known. Mira has always been overly hands-on, sticking her nose into every aspect of my life. I chalked it up to her being really vested in my career. And I had no reason to think badly of her; after all, she was instrumental in my success. But when she burrowed deeper into my life instead of backing off, I should've at least suspected there was something unhealthy in her focus on me.

My lawyers are working to terminate our contract. I can't even bear to talk to her. She's been trying to contact me, but by blocking her calls I'm making my position clear. The attorneys are also untangling the mess Mira's interference has created in Bethany's life. Given their hourly rate, they should be able to purge Mira from our lives completely. I won't accept anything less.

I start a new text to my chief publicist Christopher.

Announce to the press that Paige and I are separating on an amicable—

Damn it. I click the delete key until the text is all gone. I've been trying to make the announcement, but just haven't been able to. I'm not exactly sure what I'm hoping for. Paige isn't going to tell me she loves me, or that she's perfectly fine with how my own fucking agent endangered Bethany or threatened Renni.

"You okay?" Elliot asks.

"Yes," I say, but I don't sound convincing… even to my own ears.

"I don't mind if you want to move in, but you know that sooner or later Elizabeth is gonna march in here and drag you back to your mansion."

He's right. Elizabeth and Paige call at least five times a day. Each. Paige texts me too, but I haven't read any of the messages. I don't have the guts.

I go to the garage and hop into my Ferrari. I should find a hotel to stay at. Out of habit, I start to dial Paige to arrange a suite, then stop. She isn't my assistant, and she probably doesn't want to lift a finger on my behalf.

I've screwed up so bad.

So I stop at the first big hotel I see and toss my keys to the valet. I don't give a damn where I stay, so long as they have a room for me.

Of *course* we have a room, Mr. Reed! Would you like the presidential suite? Of course, we will be happy to, sir. Will there be anything else, sir?

Normally a cocky smile would split my face, and I'd wink at the female front desk clerk until she flushed and fluttered her eyelashes at me. The phrase "Isn't my life so fucking awesome?" would ring in my head as I took the keycard and walked away to the elevator. If she was pretty enough, I'd hint that she should come up and have a drink after her shift ended.

But now I look at the woman with about the same interest I'd show a piece of plywood. And when I take the key and walk away, the emptiness in my heart is like acid. The other guests stare at me, and it only intensifies the hollowness deep inside.

They think I have everything.

They couldn't be more wrong.

I pick up a new cap from the hotel gift shop and walk along the street. My phone's off, although it sits in my pocket. That and my plastic are all I have on me as I wander around, letting my feet take me wherever.

My gaze falls on a couple with their arms linked. The girl is a brunette, with a pair of square black librarian glasses. Her pale hand contrasts sharply against her man's olive-toned skin.

They aren't anybody famous. They aren't anybody rich. I'd bet my Ferrari they've never lived in a house with twice the number of bedrooms as people. They're just regular, everyday people, smiling and leaning into each other as they step along and share a joke.

They're happy and content.

And I'd give all I have to switch places with them.

I walk for a while and somehow end up in front of a jewelry store owned by Kiyoko Hamada, the woman who designed Paige's engagement ring. There are more exquisite items on display in the window. White pearls, diamond earrings and necklace sets sparkle under the lights. The pearls are so big and lustrous, they seem to glow from within.

When I commissioned the engagement ring, I had simple hopes for my life. A loving wife. Maybe a child or two. Most people find those attainable, but not me. To me, they're big dreams, and seem harder than flying to the moon.

Suddenly the door to the shop opens, and the last person I ever thought I'd see at a jeweler walks out. My cousin, Dane Pryce, in all his glory.

His dark hair is neatly cropped, and he's in a navy blue bespoke suit. Grimness pours off him, although it's not as bad as usual. Maybe he's mellowing in his old age.

"Dane?" I say, hardly believing it. "What are you doing here?"

The icy blue eyes narrow. "I could ask the same. Trying to stock up on peace offerings for the times you're going to screw up?"

My mood snaps from shock to pissed off. *Why do I even talk to this guy?* "You're such a fucking asshole."

"At least I don't go to strip clubs while I'm engaged. Nor am I stupid enough to get caught."

I grind my teeth. "Are you shopping for a ring?" I say, not wanting to get into my failing personal life. He has no other reason to come here. He isn't the type to give women lots of expensive jewelry just because.

Nothing changes on his face, except for the subtle color on his cheeks.

"Son of a bitch." I chuckle. "You are!"

His stare grows colder. "And you? Are you going to go in, or stand out here all day running your lips?"

"Nah. I was just out for a stroll."

"Well, exercise time is over. I'll take you to your car."

Normally I would refuse. But since my Ferrari's several miles away—much farther than he's expecting—I say, "Sure. Why not?"

Once we're both in his Bentley, I tell him where my car is. He narrows his eyes. "That's at least fifteen blocks away."

I give him my most angelic smile. "You did offer…"

He starts driving. He stays just below the speed limit, which reminds me of an octogenarian with oversized knuckles white around the steering wheel.

"What happened to your Lamborghini?" I ask.

"I got bored with it."

I raise my eyebrows. He loves that car more than anything else in the world. If he could, he would've married the thing.

"So, you and Paige are going to split," Dane says, his eyes on the road. "True, or gossip rag bullshit?"

"Jeez. Have you been stalking me?"

"Hardly. I can't get away from you." His mouth curls in distaste. "It's all over the news, for one."

I say nothing. Paige's and my situation is just too painful and raw to talk about…especially to someone like Dane, who has the emotional range of a can opener.

"So it's true." He sighs at an idiot who cuts him off. But then he shouldn't be driving like an old woman if he doesn't want to be dissed on the road. "Was it your decision?"

"Does it matter?"

"I see. Not your decision. Well, if you want her, take her."

I choke. "I'm not a rapist."

"Then convince her," he says, like I'm the biggest idiot in the world.

"Easier said than done."

"My advice," Dane says, "is to get out of L.A. Both of you are under a microscope here. Go to the family vacation home in the Maldives. Or the one in Thailand. Or Tahiti. If the idiot media follow you in a helicopter, shoot it down. That's what guards are for. Then, once you're alone with her, convince Paige that you're not a total loss." He drives on, inscrutable behind his sunglasses. "Or, second option: sit by and watch her marry some other sap, go live in a home with a white-picket fence, have two point three children and drive a gently used minivan."

I stare at him, feeling like I'm in a *Twilight Zone* episode. Getting relationship advice from Dane is like getting lessons on how to be a moral, upstanding citizen from Ted Bundy.

"They might even get a dog," Dane adds, scowling now as though that's the most offensive possibility out of all the ones he's listed.

I don't know how to respond. He's actually trying to help out. "Why are you bothering to give me advice? You don't even like me."

"Beside the point," he says.

"No, seriously. Why?"

He glances my way for a fraction of a second. "Grandma Shirley wanted me to."

"Are you kidding? Grandma Shirley hated me."

"No. She *worried* about you because you aren't particularly bright or cool-headed. Being emotional is a terrible handicap."

"Right. Because having ice water for blood is so much better." Shaking my head, I lean back in my seat. "I really want to know who you bought the ring for. I want to meet the woman who'd say yes to a man who'd be hot in an igloo."

The muscles in his jaw flex. "Worry about yourself." He stops the car in front of my hotel. "Get out."

I do. The second I slam the door shut, he drives off. I watch the Bentley slowly disappear around the block.

As much as I hate Dane, he's right about one thing. Paige is going to be snapped up by someone. And that man is going to share her bed, give her children…

My hands curl into fists. The idea of her with another man makes me want to vomit. So I need to do something here. And Dane's suggestion is a good one…plus, I was thinking about it already. Leave the country. Lie low. Have a heart-to-heart talk.

My lawyers are doing what they can to ensure that Mira isn't going to screw with Paige's stepsister or Renni. But ultimately, Paige has to know that Mira was involved in Bethany's accident, even if her influence was indirect. I don't want to have any ugly secrets between us that can come back later to bite me in the ass.

Then I should just calmly explain why she should forget what I told her about my loving her—I said that all wrong anyway—and she should give us a chance without any preconceived notions about how we should end it all.

A good plan. In fact, it's perfect.

I switch on my phone. Time to execute.

◯

Paige

I NO LONGER KNOW WHAT TO MAKE OF RYDER'S

absence. I don't think anything's happened to him; if it had, I would've seen it on the news.

One possible clue: Elliot isn't answering his phone either. Elizabeth hasn't been able to get a hold of either of her brothers, and she's convinced Elliot and Ryder are up to no good.

"One plus one isn't two when they're together. It's more like ten."

We have barely a week left before our wedding. Mom's called twice, but I told her I didn't know what was going on and asked her to not make any travel plans.

The list I made to convince Ryder that I love him too sits forlornly on my desk. At the rate things are going, I may never get a chance to use it.

Julian wanted me to ditch Ryder at the altar. It looks like it's going to be the opposite, with me left behind. *Now isn't that ironic?*

Renni texts me to see when the rehearsal is. I text back, *I don't know.*

I'm going to kill him when I see him, you know that, right?

A reluctant smile tugs at me. *Yes, but you should at least wait until you have an airtight alibi.*

You can be my alibi. This shit isn't cool, Paige. Don't let him get away with it. He's gotta respect you.

My eyes sting. I press my lips together until

they hurt. Renni means well, but she doesn't know everything that's going on between me and Ryder…or the fact that he said he loved me. I haven't told anybody about our last big fight. If I did, I'd have to talk about how I'm in love with him, too. I'm not saying that out loud to anyone until I get a chance to tell him first. He deserves at least that much.

Bethany calls me on the sixth day Ryder has been missing. Presumably she feels like it's the kind of topic you should actually talk about, rather than just texting back and forth.

It's after dinner time, and my stomach is feeling less than happy. "Hey," I say, my voice listless. I plop on the bed in my room and stare at the ceiling.

"Hi. Um…are you sick?"

"No. Just…too full from dinner. No appetite, but I ate anyway for the baby's sake."

"Oh." A bit of awkward silence. "They always make you eat a lot." She clears her throat. "Are you guys okay? Mom's kind of worried."

"I don't know." I sigh. The light from the bedside lamp hits the ring on my finger, and the bright sparkles cut my heart. "I can't get a hold of Ryder."

There is a long pause. "Just so you know, I've been in touch with his lawyers."

"About what?"

"The funding for my website. He's going to do it, rather than that trust."

"Oh. Well…that's great."

"You didn't know?" She turns it into a question, but she already knows the answer.

"We talked a bit about it, but…no. I didn't."

"The contract he offered is very fair, much better terms, and the other guy backed off without a fight."

Mira can be headstrong, but she can't win against Ryder. Not only is he her client, but underneath that carefree playboy façade lies steel.

"Anyway, I just thought I should mention it and thank you. I know you had something to do with it."

"Not at all." Her gratitude is misdirected; she only became a target because of me. She needs to know, so I tell her how Mira used the trust to get to her, in order to use her as leverage against me.

"Are you *kidding?* What a…witch!" Bethany says in outrage.

"Yup. I'm sure she'll leave you alone now, though."

"More importantly, she better leave *you* alone. You aren't some puppet she can control!"

"I know. I'm sure she's learned her lesson," I say.

A text comes in. I pause for a second. "Can you hold?" My heart pounding, I check it. *Maybe it's Ryder...* Disappointment crashes through me when I see that it's from Renni. I click on it, just in case it's something urgent. Although Mira's backed off from my stepsister, she also threatened my best friend.

I thought I should send you this before you see it on the Internet. Apparently Ryder's been staying here.

She's attached a photo of a hotel I'm familiar with. It's the place Ryder had that orgy the night before his cousin's rehearsal dinner. He's coming out of the building in the picture, eyes hidden behind a huge pair of sunglasses.

The usual assholes are saying you guys broke up, but I don't buy it. Argh. Maybe we should sue them for defamation or something, no?

I return to my call with Bethany. "I have to go. I'll talk to you later, okay?"

"Of course. Take care of yourself. And no matter what happens, just remember you're awesome and I love you."

"Love you, too, Bethany."

I go back to the picture. Then I type, *When?*

Yesterday according to the "news," Renni responds.

Thank you!

After throwing on a clean tunic and skirt, I grab my purse and car keys. It's time I go track down my fiancé and tell him how I feel.

There is a sense of déjà vu as I walk through the main entrance to the lobby. Chandeliers hang from the high, golden ceiling, and my shoes click with every step.

A young woman in a black suit stands behind the front desk, and she gives me a smooth professional smile. "Good evening, ma'am. How can I help you?"

"Can I speak to the manager on duty, please?"

"May I inquire what this is in regards to?"

"Just tell him Paige Johnson is here."

She frowns slightly, but says, "Please have a seat." She gestures at the empty couches behind me. "I'll be right back."

I sit and wait. The orchids on the table look exceptionally white and elegant. Thin but sturdy wires hold the stems in place.

Soon, the manager comes out. This time he doesn't come with security. I give him a small, friendly smile.

"Paige. What a surprise," he says, his words lightly accented.

"Hello, Patrik." I stand up. "I'm here to see Ryder. I understand he's staying here."

"Oh, terribly sorry, but Mr. Reed checked out just an hour ago."

"He did?" I say almost stupidly.

Patrik looks sympathetically devastated. "If I'd only known you were coming…"

Suddenly I'm tired. "Do I need to settle the account?"

His palms jump up between us. "No, not at all. Everything's been taken care of."

"He might've left something behind. Would you mind if I check?"

There's something that looks suspiciously like pity in his kind blue eyes. "Of course. Let me grab a keycard, and we can go up together."

We take an empty elevator. I keep my chin up and back straight even though I want to collapse in a corner and cry. Down the hall, we hit the same suite where Ryder had his wild party with naked women and empty bottles of booze and the hazy smoke of burnt pot.

Housekeeping hasn't had a chance to clean the suite yet. I turn to Patrik. "You don't have to stay. It may take a while."

He nods and steps back a pace. "Take your time."

The door closes behind him with a soft click.

I look around. No signs of wild partying or womanizing. Just rumpled sheets and a shower that's been used. A couple of towels on the bathroom floor. I kneel on the side of the bed and bury my face in the pillows.

They smell like Ryder—the clean soap and that indefinable man scent that never fails to send hot jitters of longing thorough my whole being. The pain of not having him with me is almost physical, a knife piercing my heart. I press a tight fist against my chest and swallow a sob.

I fumble through my purse until I find my phone. I dial Ryder's number. He used to always answer me, but now…

This time is no exception. After what feels like forever, I get voice mail.

"You have reached…" a soulless mechanical voice drones on until a sharp beep cuts it off.

"Ryder, it's me. Paige. I don't know where you are…or how angry you still are with me, but I want you to know I miss you and I want you back. You remember how you said I was looking forward to the end of one year? Well, you were wrong. I was afraid. I just couldn't believe you could ever love me, and I didn't want to be that cliché—an assistant who falls for her boss. But…" I drag in a shuddery breath. Hot tears thicken in my throat, and I compose myself so I can actually talk rather than start blubbering like an idiot. "I'm in love with you, Ryder. Crazy, stupid in love. It hurts to be away from you, and I hope it's not too late for us. Just come back. I'm so sorry about everything. I—"

The voice mail beeps again, ending the recording. My hand clenches around my phone. And this time I can't stop the flow of tears or the sounds of sorrow and loss being dragged out from deep inside me.

By the time I leave the suite, the pillows are soaked through.

TWENTY-FIVE

Paige

I DO NOT WANT TO GET UP THE NEXT MORNING. Nor do I want to go downstairs and sit at the counter with Elizabeth and pretend to be okay.

The mirror presents a horror show. Red rims my swollen eyes, and my complexion is blotchy. If it weren't for being pregnant, I'd just stay in bed. But I have to think about the baby.

With a sigh, I put on a t-shirt and a pair of gray sweats and drag myself downstairs. Sue, the housekeeper, puts sunny yellow daisies in the living room and dining room…maybe to counteract my mood. I'm not exactly good at masking my emotions.

Elizabeth, of course, looks perfect. She's at the counter, outfitted impeccably in a blue designer dress, sipping her coffee as usual. Her eyes go dark with concern and worry as she looks at me. "Are you all right?"

"Yeah." My voice is a rasp, and I wince.

"I'm such an idiot. Of course you aren't okay. When he comes back, I'm going to kill him. Then handcuff him to you." She gestures at the counter. "The chef made some eggs, bacon and pancakes. If you'd rather have something else—"

"No, it's fine." The chef could offer me a gold-plated, Michelin three-star pancake, and I still wouldn't want it. I'm only eating for the baby.

We sit in silence as I mechanically shovel food into my mouth. I don't want to be rude, but I also don't want to go on and on about Ryder to his sister. She doesn't seem to know what topic to safely broach either.

Maybe I should go home to Sweet Hope… or take a short trip to someplace nobody knows me…

Sue bustles in. Her face is flushed, and excitement glitters in her eyes. "It's him!"

"Who?" Elizabeth says.

"Mr. Reed!"

I jump to my feet. "He's here?"

"No. He sent a car for you." She flings her arm behind her. "You're supposed to pack a few things and go with the driver as soon as possible."

I don't even bother to hear the rest of what she has to say. Food forgotten, I rush to my suite and start packing. Since I have no idea how long it's going to be or anything, I toss fistfuls of everything into a suitcase.

Elizabeth comes in a few minutes later. "Make sure you take your passport as well," she says. "And only your lightest clothes."

"Why?" I ask, not stopping.

"Because." Her smile reaches her eyes, and their corners crinkle. "The driver told me you're going to Thailand."

That stops me. "*Thailand?*"

"Uh-huh. Our family—on the Pryce side, I mean—has a vacation home there. Very private." She shakes her head. "That must be where he is, although I have no idea why. It's so far away."

"I don't care how far it is. I'm going! Now!"

She laughs at my enthusiasm. "Okay, okay." She removes a pair of sweats from my suitcase, along with two long-sleeved shirts. "Don't forget to send a postcard."

I scurry around, gathering all my shorts and light tops and hurling them into the suitcase. One of the men who maintain the garden at the mansion comes up, takes my bag downstairs and loads it into the waiting Mercedes.

Finally! I'll see Ryder in a few hours.

The ride to the airport feels interminable. I clasp my hands together, then let them go, and squirm around. Sitting still like a grown-up is impossible. I feel like a kid on Christmas Eve.

Ryder's pristine white jet is waiting. I walk up the steps to board, then step inside the cabin. There's an attendant…but that's it.

"Where's Ryder?" I ask the woman.

"You're the only passenger."

My mouth parts. "I am?"

"Yes, ma'am. Please sit down and relax. Would you like anything to drink? Ginger ale? We also have various juices, water…"

"No." I shake my head, taking a seat. "I'm all right."

Except I'm not all right. I was so certain Ryder was going to join me. He could've left last night, but then why didn't he take his plane?

For all I know, Ryder may be staying in L.A., and banishing me to the opposite end of the planet. I pull out my phone in case he's left a text or a voice mail. But there's nothing.

I don't even know if he's heard my message. Sudden fatigue weighs me down, and as the plane starts to taxi I lay my head listlessly against the leather seat and close my eyes.

Ryder

Dane may be an asshole—no, he *is* an asshole—but he's an honest one. I inspect the vacation home, making sure it's perfect. The beach is so clean it looks almost artificial. The water is a perfect shade of aquamarine, and the white sand feels like silk between my bare toes. Not a cloud mars the endless blue of the sky, and the breeze helps cool me down some, although I must admit the humidity is brutal. Having lived in L.A. for so long, the mugginess is killing me.

But it's a small sacrifice to pay for privacy. I stopped by the market, just as a test, and the locals didn't pull out their phones to snap photos or start following me around. They checked me out—after all I'm a foreigner—but they left me alone otherwise. And the shop clerks were sweet without fawning over me.

I hate to admit it, but Dane's suggestion was spot-on. This is exactly the kind of place Paige and I need to spend some time if we want to work out our issues.

The housekeeper, Peeraya, comes out of the house. "Sir, you have message from the airport. Madam's plane landed," she says, her lilting accent softening every syllable. "She will come soon."

"Thank you." I turn, facing the beach again.

The phone in my pocket seems to grow heavier. I know there's a new voice mail from Paige, but I'm not going to listen to it. I can't.

What if she said, "I'm sorry you love me. That was never what I wanted"? Then I'd have to abort this whole mission. But not knowing, I can still cling to hope.

Closing my eyes, I breathe in the ocean air. If she were any other woman, I would've known she was sending me a voice mail fawning over me. Perhaps her refusal to be dazzled by my money and fame is what makes Paige so interesting and lovable. I know that even if I lost everything, she wouldn't treat me any different. To her, I'm always going to be just Ryder.

But I want to be Ryder *the Man She Loves*.

Soon the black SUV shows up. I see a shadow in the back seat.

My heart thumps once, a powerful knock against my ribs, then starts racing. My mouth goes dry.

This is it. The moment I lay down everything.

I go out and open the door for her, while the driver takes her suitcase. In a light white sundress, Paige smells fresh, like soap and floral shampoo; clearly, she used the amenities on the jet. I have to reign myself in from inhaling her and kissing her until we're both breathless and needy. As awesome as sex is, it's not going to give me what I really need right now—her heart.

Dark circles show underneath her concealer, and her eyes are slightly puffy. "Was the flight bad?" I ask. She should've had a bed to herself to sleep.

"No, it was great. I just, you know…couldn't really sleep much." Her gaze roams over me like she can't believe it. Hopefully she's not thinking, "I can't believe he dragged me out here."

My hand at the small of her back, I escort her to the house. The foyer is airy with a tall ceiling and lots of glass. The living room is the same, and it has a spectacular view of the ocean.

The dining room smells amazing. Peeraya has laid out huge fried prawns and dipping sauces as an appetizer, salads and a shallow pot with two fresh bass simmered in a mild broth spiced with Thai herbs.

"Want something to eat?" I ask.

"Are you hungry?" she says instead.

I realize I am. "Yeah."

"Then let's eat."

She washes her hands and returns to the dining room. I pull out a chair for her, and she sits down.

I take the chair across from her. "Start with the shrimp."

"I've never eaten anything like this before." She picks one up, looking slightly worried.

"Yeah, it's not your typical American breaded and fried shrimp." For one, the prawn is huge, almost the size of Paige's hand. It's been wrapped in some kind of thin noodles and fried. The noodle wrapping is dry and crispy, while the shrimp is warm and juicy inside.

She takes a few bites, then stops, licking her lips. "Ryder… Did you get my message?"

"Yes," I say, my gut suddenly tight. I reach for my water.

"I want you to know I meant everything."

"Paige, I —"

The tears gathering in the corners of her eyes stop me short. Looking up, she blinks hard. "I don't even know why I'm crying like this." She fans herself. "I'm being so silly."

"No, you aren't." I swallow, gather my courage. "I got it…but I haven't listened to it yet."

She starts. "You haven't?"

"No, I… Look. I have to tell you something first."

"Okay." Her voice is shaky.

"I fired Mira."

"What?

"Yeah. I did." I forge on, needing to get it all out before my nerves get the best of me. "Nobody can hurt you—or the people you care about—and get away with it."

"But Ryder…she's your agent!"

"Yes, and you're my fiancée. And I told you which one matters more."

Paige gazes at me, then nods slowly. "So you did. I guess I should start believing you, huh?"

"Yes. Please do believe me." I get out of my chair and kneel by her side, taking her free hand in both of mine. The skin-to-skin contact feels so good, I close my eyes to savor it for a moment. "I was wrong and stupid all along. You said I didn't treat you like you were my fiancée, and you were right. I didn't. I treated you like you were an extra in my movie. I should've listened to what you wanted, what was important to you."

"Ryder…"

"We're going to elope, just like you wanted. Who gives a shit about putting on a show? I thought I could give you up and find somebody else, but I can't. I love you. I've never said it to any woman before, not even to Lauren. Something always held me back…until you."

More tears bead in her eyes, and this time she lets them fall. I wipe them away, my fingers clumsy and desperate. I'm worse than Dane. Not even he would make the love of his life cry.

I speak fast. I need to get it all out before she makes her decision. "Paige, we can have a year together, and if you decide that I'm not the one you want, then…" *My heart will shrivel and never recover.* I lick my lips, which have gone completely dry. "Then you can get rid of me. But until that time comes, give me a chance to earn your love. I'm not as bad as the media says. If you want, we can live here for a year, away from the spotlight and—"

She puts a hand over my mouth.

All the air stills in my body, and I remain frozen. I'm at the edge of a cliff, blindfolded and teetering. Either I'm going to be pushed into the abyss or I'm going to be saved. I just don't know which option Paige is going to choose.

"If you'd listened to my message, you crazy man, you would've known I love you," she says. "You would've known I was waiting for you to come home and that I missed you so much."

A dam inside me bursts, and I start shaking. It's as though all the fear and doubt pours out of me, leaving nothing but joy and happiness in their wake.

With a loud whoop, I pull her in for a kiss. She responds immediately, her lips open, her tongue thrusting inside, and her teeth trapping my lower lip so I can't retreat.

Desire boils my blood even as I cradle Paige's face in my hands. Our lips are fused, our heartbeats synchronizing. I feel like we're becoming a single unit that is greater than the sum of two people.

She pulls back and glances at the dinner table. "You think all this will still be okay if we microwave it later?"

"Most definitely."

A wicked smile splits her face. "Then show me your room."

TWENTY-SIX

Paige

RYDER CARRIES ME TO THE SECOND LEVEL, HIS eyes brilliant with desire. I clutch his wide shoulders, feeling the powerful muscles underneath the shirt. I'm almost afraid this is a dream, and I'm going to wake up and find myself alone in my room. My heart beats like it's going to burst out of my chest, and I kiss him like I want to inhale him so he'll always be a part of me.

In his room he puts me down. We are still kissing; he gently pushes me backward until my calves hit the cool wooden bed frame. My hands clutch him as the world slowly tilts…and then I'm on my back on the sheets, my legs dangling over the edge, knees bent.

Ryder rises up over me, his handsome face tight with need. Stepping out of his shoes, he takes off his clothes, the movements graceful. The muscles on his body are hard and strong, honed with meticulous care. My mouth parts. It's hard to believe such a perfect man is mine.

Heat pulses through me as he strips my dress and underwear off with shaking hands. Everywhere his calloused fingers graze, goosebumps follow, leaving me shivery and weak with longing. I pull his face down for a kiss, my fingers tunneling into the warm silk of his hair.

Our tongues tangle, our mouths mold against each other, greedy and desperate. The kiss feels different now—sweeter and freeing. It's as though all the barriers are gone, no fear or hesitation holding us back.

"You're gorgeous," he groans, running his lips down my neck, his breath fanning my hypersensitive skin. I feel it all the way to my core.

He plumps my breast in one large hand, weighing and studying the shape. He rolls the nipple between his fingers, and sensation hits me like a lightning bolt. I cry out, my back arching.

His mouth curves into the cockeyed grin that has broken millions of female hearts around the world. But not mine. Unlike the movies, there's love in his eyes, direct and unconditional and true.

"Perfect." He pulls the nipple into his mouth.

His cheeks hollow as he sucks hard, and pleasure makes my skin prickle until I can barely lie still.

I'm so slick—dripping between my thighs. He drags the sensitive tip until it pops out of his mouth wetly. I whimper at the sharp pleasure.

He subjects the other nipple to the same erotic torture. It's as though there's a direct link between my nipples and my clit. I can feel every suck, every nip all the way to that tiny bundle of nerves.

Gently, he guides my hand between my legs. "Make yourself feel good," he says against my hard, wet nipple. His warm breath on the sensitive peak has my blood boiling, and I cry out softly.

My eyes on his, I touch myself. My fingertips are immediately drenched, and he's back to tormenting my oversensitive breasts. I rub my swollen clit; waves of electric pleasure ripples through me, and a sheen of sweat spreads over my tingling skin. But it's not enough.

I pull away from him and move up on the bed. "I want you inside me, Ryder."

"Happy to oblige. And I want to hear you come with my name on your lips."

"It's not about my pleasure," I say. "It's about us connecting in the most intimate way a man and a woman can. I want to feel you all the way inside me." I cradle his heartbreakingly handsome face in my hands. "Don't deny me. Please."

His forehead touches mine. "I could never deny you."

Bracing himself on his elbows, he positions himself between my legs. I spread my thighs, eager and waiting. He pushes inside, slowly, inch by agonizing inch. I brace my feet on the bed and tilt my hips in encouragement.

Our gazes lock. I feel like I'm peering into his soul as he hilts himself in me.

"God, you're perfect," he groans.

"So are you."

"I can't believe you're mine."

"I'm all yours," I whisper. "Forever."

He pulls out and drives in. Every stroke rubs against the sensitive interior nerves, and with every thrust I sink a little bit deeper into a universe of pleasure. My hands dig into the strong muscles of his back, slick with sweat, and his name is a loving chant on my lips.

Ryder shifts the angle of his pelvis, rolling his hips. Now his thrusts hit my clit as well, and my toes start to curl.

"Come for me, Paige. Come with me."

His voice rasps over my senses. Everything inside me coils tightly until—

I let go. I know he'll always be there to catch me.

Tendons stand out on his neck as he joins me, his cock lodged deep inside. Just watching the pleasure twisting through him sends the sweetest ache through me, and I can't help but bring his head down for a soul-deep kiss.

"Thank you," he says against my lips when he can catch his breath.

"For what?"

He presses his mouth to my forehead. His voice is quiet when he says, "For completing me."

It takes one more day to get our marriage license. Apparently Ryder hired local lawyers, who did what they had to to expedite the process.

"We don't have to do it today if you don't want to," he says as we share breakfast in bed. Peeraya has prepared omelets and whole wheat toast, plus freshly squeezed mango and pineapple juice.

Since my appetite is back with a vengeance, I stuff my face with another bite of eggs and shake my head. After I wash it down with the juice, I say, "I do want to. Let's do it."

"You sure? Don't you want to walk down the aisle with Simon?"

"I do, but maybe we can have another small ceremony or something when we get back home." I squeeze his hand, then shoot him a sassy grin.

"Besides, I have another, slightly vindictive reason for wanting to marry ASAP."

He cocks an eyebrow.

"Julian. He threatened me."

Ryder's eyes narrow.

I bump his shoulder with mine. "Don't worry. I won't try to solve the problem on my own. But he does want to keep that painting that's rightfully yours. So I'm going to do everything in my power to spite him. I might even set your siblings up with potential spouses." I'm not a big fan of Ryder's father. I'm not going to let him win. No way.

"Getting Grandpa's portrait is going to be great, no doubt, but having you is worth more." He kisses me on the forehead. "Even if Julian reneges on giving us the paintings, I'll still be happy because I have you."

I flush with pleasure and love. Ryder really says the most romantic things. He should've been a screenwriter. He could've made a name for himself churning out romance scripts.

In the morning, while it's still relatively cool, the staff builds a huge arch entwined with gorgeous purple and white tropical orchids. I step outside to admire the setup. The orchids sweeten the ocean air's tang with a tropical floral fragrance. I've never smelled anything so divine.

We're going to have a sunset ceremony. I go through my suitcase for something appropriate. I don't think I can do a bikini wedding, even though I saw one on the Internet. I'm still a little more traditional than that.

Thankfully, I somehow remembered to pack a cute strapless white dress. It has a simple sweetheart bodice and a chiffon skirt that reaches my knees. Josephine bought it for our engagement party in case I didn't feel like wearing the "ribbon on the back" dress. She's a firm believer of buying two outfits for every event because you never know.

"What if you spill red wine on your first choice?" she asked blithely as she tossed the dress on top of the "buy" pile. "Think about it."

Even though I'm more pregnant, the clothes still fit me okay, and Peeraya magically produces a pair of white pumps with one and a half inch heels that are not only comfortable but fairy tale princess beautiful with tiny white beads and lace.

"You are *awesome*," I tell her, beaming.

"I'm glad you're happy, madam." She smiles back.

About two hours before the ceremony, she brings in a basket full of beautiful white flowers whose names I don't know.

"They are from the garden. Perfect for you."

Perfect for me? I wonder, but it soon becomes clear as she directs me to sit down in front of a huge vanity. Her talented hands weave the blossoms into my curled hair, one by one, then set them in place with pins. When she's done, I look like some kind of tropical paradise goddess.

The sun sinks slowly into the ocean, and everything becomes drenched in reddish gold.

The local violinists start "Here comes the bride."

It's time.

At the makeshift altar stands a British ex-pat minister who is going to officiate our wedding. Ryder stands by the arch to the left. A classic black tux fits him perfectly, from the powerful V of his lean torso to the strong thighs. The breeze from the Andaman Sea ruffles his hair, and his eyes sparkle like stars.

There are people who want to keep us apart, and I'm not talking about the faceless masses. There's Julian, who's going to be furious. And I doubt Mira is going to just go quietly into the sunset.

But none of that matters now, because I'm here with Ryder. We can fight the entire planet together if need be.

I take a step forward to my future.

Happiness and bone-deep contentment rise within me like champagne bubbles. I am exactly where I belong—a Hollywood bride to the love of my life.

TWENTY-SEVEN

Elliot

I'VE BEEN TO A LOT OF STRIP CLUBS, AND I'VE watched a lot of women putting their assets on display.

But this girl on stage…

Her face is pretty enough. Klieg lights glint off too red hair, and a heavy layer of makeup enlarges her green eyes and gives her mouth that "ready to suck a dick" look.

Underneath all the artifice, though, she's got something. A quality I haven't seen in the others.

Too bad she's the worst stripper I've ever seen in my life.

It's not her body. Her tits are big and bouncy—probably real—and firm from youth. Her ass is round and taut and would be a great double-handful to grab when I thrust into her warm, wet pussy—the thought of which makes my cock swell with interest.

But she has zero moves.

Stripping is like fucking. A guy can have the biggest dick in the world, but if he has no idea what to do with it, he might as well have no dick at all.

I turn away, but the girl's awkwardness tugs something at me, and I feel bad for her. She's obviously new and has no talent for the work even though she's doing her best to imitate what the other girls have done before her.

When she comes my way, I sigh and stick a couple hundred-dollar bills under the tight string of her thong. Even in the dim lighting, her expression makes it clear that she knows they're a mercy tip. At least she isn't stupid.

"You really should get another gig. This just isn't your calling," I tell her.

I guess it's not really kosher to point out a lack of stripping talent. The girl looks murderous as she glares at me.

I wonder if she's going to slap me. That would liven things up…

But she doesn't. Despite her total lack of talent in stripping, she apparently has some professionalism.

I watch her walk away, almost tripping over her shoes. What the fuck is wrong with me that I'm almost disappointed she didn't try to slap me?

Look for Elliot's story, *An Improper Deal*, later this summer. Sign up for Nadia 's new release mailing list at http://www.nadialee.net/newsletter to be notified when it's out!

ABOUT NADIA LEE

NEW YORK TIMES AND USA TODAY BESTSELLING author Nadia Lee writes sexy, emotional contemporary romance. Born with a love for excellent food, travel and adventure, she has lived in four different countries, kissed stingrays, been bitten by a shark, ridden an elephant and petted tigers.

Currently, she shares a condo overlooking a small river and sakura trees in Japan with her husband and son. When she's not writing, she can be found reading books by her favorite authors or planning another trip.

To learn more about Nadia and her projects, please visit www.nadialee.net. To receive updates about upcoming works from Nadia, please visit www.nadialee.net to subscribe to her new release alert.

Made in the USA
Monee, IL
11 March 2024